DATE DUE

21	MAR 2	JUN 12
26	MAY 26	MAR 19
7	JAN 30	APR 13
FEB 26	MAY 17	AUG 1 7 1995
MAR 24	OCT 27	MAY 1 9 1998
FEB 11	APR 4	FEB 2 5 1999
MAR 4	AUG 13	DEC 0 4 2000
SEP 13	JUL 25	FEB 1 6 2001
JUN 22	OCT 1	MAR 0 2 2001
AUG 9	NOV 11	
FEB 10	AUG 23	JUL 2 3 2001
		7-6-02

PRINTED IN U.S.A.

Reese.   81061

Weapon heavy.

Public Library

St. Joseph, Michigan

1. Books may be kept two weeks and may be renewed once for the same period, except 7 day books and magazines.

2. A fine is charged for each day a book is not returned according to the above rule. No book will be issued to any person incurring such a fine until it has been paid.

3. All injuries to books beyond reasonable wear and all losses shall be made good to the satisfaction of the Librarian.

4. Each borrower is held responsible for all books charged on his card and for all fines accruing on the same.

WEAPON HEAVY.

JOHN REESE

DOUBLEDAY & COMPANY, INC.

GARDEN CITY, NEW YORK

1973

All of the characters in this book
are purely fictional, and any resemblance
to actual persons, living or dead,
is coincidental.

First Edition

ISBN: 0-385-08950-3
Library of Congress Catalog Card Number 72–89344
Copyright © 1973 by John Reese
All Rights Reserved
Printed in the United States of America

For old times' sake, to
GENE C. WALKER,
this book is dedicated.

CHAPTER ONE

A rider was coming toward him through the rain, sitting sidewise in the saddle, head almost covered by his slicker. Hewitt pulled his three-horse team to a stop, and waited.

The oncoming horse saw them in time, and stopped. The rider came out of his oilskin shell. "Hi, you! It's some wet, ain't it?" he said, cheerfully. A nondescript cowboy, probably broke and jobless, with the rugged and illogical optimism of so many of his hard-working craft.

"If it isn't," said Hewitt, "it'll do till it gets wet."

The cowboy enviously studied the tight house wagon. He grinned at Hewitt, who sat in relative comfort under an awning on the seat in front. "You-all air really fixed up good, ain't you?" he said.

Hewitt smiled. "I think so. Where you headed?"

"Anyplace except Dunsmuir, Kansas, U. S. of A.!"

"How far am I from Dunsmuir?"

"Skeercely a mile. You'd see it by now, if it wasn't raining so hard. Not that there's much to see."

"Not much of a town, I take it."

"Eight thousand cows waiting for railroad cars. No feed closer than five, six miles, and it's going fast. If you work for the Fishhook outfit, hit's a good town."

"Only you didn't."

"Not by a damn' sight!" the cowboy said. "Danged rich outfits, you might as well be on a prison chain gang." He studied the handsome sign on the house wagon:

The One and Only
JEFFERSON HEWITT
Mr. Fix-It, Himself!
REPAIRS: Household wares, pots & pans etc., made like new, unique combination of solder and rivets. Finest cabinet work & furniture restoration. Locksmith.
PORTRAIT ARTIST: Your likeness in permanent oil crayon, done in the privacy of your own home. The ideal gift for your loved ones!
HEALING MASSAGE: Jefferson Hewitt treats stiff or painful Rheumatic Joints by manipulation. Painless! No charge unless you are relieved of your agony.
THE ONE AND ONLY: Many imitations, but only one
JEFFERSON HEWITT

The cowboy, studying the man under the awning, saw an average-looking man of average size and indeterminate age. Good boots and good brown serge pants showed under his fine slicker. Expensive black hat with cavalry crease. Necktie and white shirt showing at the throat.

Jefferson Hewitt's face was lean, knotty, neither handsome nor ugly. Hazel eyes that did not disclose his thoughts. Short, heavy mustache—brown, with a reddish cast. Under it, the mouth was large, but straight, firm and decisive, and perhaps a little hard.

"Wrong season of the year to hit Dunsmuir," the cowboy said. "Town is splittin' at the seams. That's why I'm gettin' out with my summer's pay, while I still got it. They'll pick your bones and then sell the bones, mister!"

"Thank you. I'll try to take care of myself."

The cowboy grinningly pulled his slicker up to cover his face, and rode on. Hewitt's team moved ahead eagerly, at a twitch of the lines. Tied behind the wagon was a fourth horse. All four were handsome chestnuts.

Hewitt passed a sign saying, WELCOME TO DUNSMUIR, THE TOWN THAT INVENTED HOSPITALITY. Suddenly there it was, veiled by a driving sheet of rain—a single street, with buildings only on one side, in a sea of mud. On the other side of the street lay the side tracks and main line of the railroad, beyond them, the stockyards and loading chutes.

The single business street seemed to be several blocks long. After he had crossed the tracks, Hewitt could see a few short side streets with houses and a few trees, as far from the tracks as they could get.

The town that had invented hospitality seethed with stag men, all wearing the cowpuncher's working clothes. Hewitt let his team pick its gait down the main street through the mud, letting them study his smart, weather-proof rig. The plank sidewalks were sheltered by roofs. One, two, three, four blocks of men jammed in under the roof, disconsolately waiting for a change in the weather.

There was one saloon in each block. Hitchrails were full, horses standing knee-deep in mud. A few wagons, buckboards and spring wagons.

He passed a hotel—the Devlin House, a name that made Hewitt smile to himself. That name, Devlin, awoke some disturbing memories, but he was not likely to find that Devlin here. It was a good-looking building with a big, well-lighted lobby. Looked new and well-run, a money-maker.

In the next block there was another big, new building, with a huge, gaudy red-and-white sign over it:

Devlin's
ROYAL BAR AND SALOON

The crowd in front of the Royal parted suddenly, as the big double doors opened. A rowdy cowboy was being ejected, but not by bouncers. Hewitt caught his breath and reined in his horses, as he saw a tall, buxom woman in a chaste white dress with a high white collar, steering the inebriated cowhand.

"Go back to camp and sober up, Shorty," she was saying, in a clear, good-natured contralto. "You can't misbehave in my place, and you know it!"

"Aw, look, ma'am it's raining!" the cowboy said.

"It'll sober you up. You can stand a bath anyway. Now you go on, Shorty—be nice!"

Her heavy mass of red-blond hair was piled high in a convoluted mass of braids. Her skin was so white it seemed to glow. Hewitt could not see her eyes, but he knew how blue they were.

He shook the lines over the horses and turned his face so the woman could not see it, as he drove on. The rage that rose at this unexpected sight of her was easy to control. Not quite so easy to suppress was the old, wild excitement.

And yet, Hewitt thought, I know better. Lordie, nobody on earth knows better than me! Now, this may complicate things. Must give this some careful thought . . .

The big livery barn with its corrals and sheds was at the end of the street. Hewitt's four horses, veteran travelers all, shot their ears forward eagerly as he turned them through the gate. A gaunt man in ragged clothing ran out of the stable, holding up both hands.

"Just keep goin'. Turn right around and go on outside. We're full up," he called.

He went back inside. Hewitt wrapped the lines and jumped down. He was only a step behind the man, going into the office in the corner of the stable. Hewitt touched his shoulder.

"Excuse me, but I take it that you're a family man, sir," he said.

The stableman faced him sullenly. "What of it?"

"How many children have you, may I ask?"

"Five, if it's any of your business."

"There are always a couple of box stalls, held back for the influential patron. The influential patron, sir, has arrived," Hewitt said, holding up a ten-dollar gold piece.

"I only work here, mister, and even a poor man has his pride. I don't take no tips," the stableman said.

"A tip is a dime. Ten dollars, sir, is a bribe," said Hewitt. "I'm sure that Elsie and Paul Devlin own this place. You'll be in no trouble, for putting up my teams. I'll talk to Elsie, and fix it up immediately."

The stableman took the coin. "If you know them well enough to know that Elsie's the boss, you can make your bluff good. I'll take care of your teams."

"May I ask your name, sir?"

"George Carrington."

"Friend George, I want my teams cleaned, rubbed dry, and grained. I want them grained lightly, and watered, twice a day. I want my wagon stored where it can be watched day and night. There's a dollar a day in it for you, over and above the bill. I suppose the Devlins' hotel has the best beds in town?"

"If you could get in. Only you can't."

"I'll get in, all right."

Carrington smiled. "I reckon maybe you will, but watch yourself! Town's full of rowdies, in a bad mood."

Hewitt unbuttoned his slicker. He wore no jacket under it. A .45 in a short, specially made holster was jammed under the belt that held his pants, tilted so that the butt was just inside the opening of the slicker.

"You might do somebody a favor if you passed the word that I won't stand for horseplay," he said. "Is there a sheriff in town?"

"No. This ain't a county seat. Got a marshal."

"The Devlins own him too?"

Carrington smiled again. "Some may think so, but I don't. Ernie Hall don't take orders from nobody."

"Do you happen to know a cowboy by the name of Charley Kenyon? Tall, skinny kid, kind of humped over, never says much. Skinny, pointed, mean face."

"Never heard the name of Kenyon. Description will fit a lot of toughs here."

Hewitt merely nodded. "I'll have the hotel send down for my valise. You'll find it under the seat of my rig. I thank you for your courtesies, friend George, and please give my warmest regards to your fine family."

It was almost dark when he left the stable. He had to feel his way through mud to where the plank sidewalk began. Almost at once, he was caught in a mob of sullen, short-tempered men who had no place to go except back to a sodden, cold, miserable cow camp.

He made his way through them, murmuring politely, "Excuse me. Please excuse me. Excuse me, please!" They made way for him and ignored him.

At the doors of the Royal, it was not a crowd, but a mob. He had almost passed it when he stopped, catching his breath sharply at sight of a single man leaning against the building, indifferent to the press of men around him.

Why, that could be my man, first thing, he thought. I'll bet it is. First Elsie, and then him. Why, this is Old Home Week indeed . . . !

A tall youth leaned against the wall near the window, thumbs tucked into his belt, eyes staring blindly at nothing. He was little more than a boy, with silky blond whiskers on a thin, chinless face. His small, tight mouth was half open over bad teeth. His sleepy eyes under his pale eyebrows were light blue in color, and without warmth.

Hewitt veered toward the window, murmuring apologies as he elbowed through the crowd. The youth paid no attention as Hewitt came close to him. The light from the window illuminated his face brightly. There could be no mistake—the waxy skin stretched taut over small bones, the three deep worry-puckers between the eyes, the small, flat nose.

Old hand that he was, Hewitt could not help but feel a sharp quiver of excitement to find himself so close to

Charley Kenyon at last. He turned his back on the youth to think it over.

Another sharp twitch of excitement went through him as he studied the interior of the Royal. There they both were, after five years! Five very prosperous years, if Hewitt was any judge.

Paul Devlin was behind the bar, superintending the bartenders. A big, portly man, handsome and well-dressed, he moved with the ponderous stride and wore the dignified expression of a born leader of men.

Hewitt knew that Paul Devlin was a hollow shell, an errand boy for his wife. The acquisitive avarice in this couple belonged to the woman with the white skin shining above a prim white dress, there on the high cashier's stool. You've put on a little weight, Elsie, Hewitt thought. The fat of the land—that's what it will do to you . . .

One thing at a time. He put the Devlins out of his mind and turned back to the kid he was sure was Charley Kenyon. He jostled hard against him, bringing the heel of his boot down on the kid's toe.

The kid came awake like a striking snake. "Where the hell do you think you're going?" he snarled.

Hewitt slid his .45 out and jammed it into the kid's stomach. "Don't worry, I know where I'm going. Do you?" he said softly. "I'll tell you, if you don't. Back to Broken Bow, Nebraska, that's where!"

He saw the kid freeze, saw the madness of terror come into his eyes. Hewitt holstered the .45 under his slicker before anyone had a chance to see it.

"Think about it, Charley Kenyon," he said.

He was half a block away before the kid caught up with

him. "Hey, what did you call me? My name is Black, Tom Black," he said.

"Sure, sure!" Hewitt kept walking.

The kid hurried along beside him. "You got me mixed up with somebody else. What the hell you trying to start?"

Hewitt stopped and faced him. "I don't make mistakes, Kenyon, but I'll think it over, and you do the same. We can talk about it later, but keep one thing in mind: If I have to kill you, kid, you'll be my fifth!"

He pushed on without looking back. Charley Kenyon for sure, he told himself, and the other one won't be far away . . . He hurried up the steps of the Devlin House and opened the door. The desk clerk saw him coming.

"No rooms, sir!" he said stridently. "No use asking, because we have no rooms."

Hewitt leaned against the desk. "Got a clean sheet of paper, sir, or a small square of white cardboard?"

"See what I can find, but one thing I can't do is give you a room," the harried clerk replied.

He took some papers from a drawer. Hewitt chose one and took four crayons from his pocket. He swiftly drew an ornate frame, in green swirls. Inside it, he wrote in red, in a flourishing hand that he shaded with black and green:

Please Replace Pen in Penholder.
Thank You!

"That will save you some trouble and give you some style, sir. Every good hotel needs one," he said.

"That's really slick, but I can't pay you for it. I didn't ask you to do it."

"No charge, but a good hotel always holds back a good room or two, for influential late guests. I am an influential late guest. Ask Elsie Devlin."

"Oh, did Mrs. Devlin send you here?"

"No, but she'll want me to have a good room, and please send someone to the livery stable for my luggage. And have a drink on me, sir."

A five-dollar gold piece twinkled across the desk. The clerk whisked it into his pocket. "Number 12, at the top of the stairs. One of the best rooms we have. I do hope Mrs. Devlin approves of this!"

"So do I," said Hewitt.

He took the key and ran lightly up the stairs, locking the door of number 12 behind him and leaving the key half-turned in the lock. It was a big room overlooking the street. He crossed it in the dark and pulled the blinds over both windows. He opened both closet doors and examined them, by feel, in the dark.

Satisfied that he was alone he lighted both big lamps. He opened the dampers on the chimney heater, to warm up the room, and hung his slicker in the closet. He put his .45 and holster on the dresser and undressed, slowly and wearily, to his long underwear. Under his shirt, he wore a .32 in a shoulder holster. He put both gun and holster on the dresser beside the .45.

Someone knocked at his door. "Bellboy, Mr. Hewitt, with your valise."

Hewitt crossed the room swiftly on bare feet. He snicked the key around and stepped aside as he flung the door open. In the hall, an old, broken-down cowboy blinked unstartled at him through a mass of frowsy gray whiskers.

"You're a mite sudden about the way you open doors, Mr. Hewitt," he said.

"A habit of mine," Hewitt said, smilingly. "Put it on the stand at the foot of the bed, please. Now, think you can find me a dozen good cigars somewhere? Real ten-centers."

"I could try."

Hewitt handed him two silver dollars. "Do! I like to know my neighbors. How are you called?"

"Bob Kramer, but nobody pays no 'tention to my last name. I'm just old Bob around here."

"You've had better jobs than this, Mr. Kramer."

The old bellboy said stiffly, "Hell is full of men who had better jobs when they was young, and wouldn't take worse ones when they got old. I eat regular and I'm in out of the weather most of the time."

"Life is what we make it, isn't it? But you'll pardon me for knowing instantly that you were no ordinary hotel flunky. Now let's have those cigars, please."

When old Bob returned with them, Hewitt handed him one before taking one for himself. Hewitt himself lighted both cigars from the same match.

"Not bad at all, Mr. Kramer."

"Mr. Hewitt, by God you're a gentleman!"

Old Bob walked a little straighter when he left. Hewitt, who carefully kept score on such things because his life might depend on it, now had two friends in town—George Carrington, the stableman, and this old hotel bell-hop, Bob Kramer.

He also had two enemies, Charley Kenyon and Elsie Devlin. Or two and a half, if you included Paul Devlin.

Hewitt unlocked his suitcase and took out a gray wool dressing gown lined with red silk. He put it on over his underwear, sat down at the dresser-desk, and took out a sheet of hotel stationery.

He drew a quick pen-and-ink sketch of the chinless youth who called himself Tom Black, shading it just enough to suggest the skull-like look of witless evil in the face. Taking up another sheet of paper, he wrote:

Dear Mr. Batchelder:

If the enclosed picture is Kenyon, I have found him. This is a shipping railhead and he probably works for a cow outfit. Slim Gurkey will be working for the same one. How to smoke them out is not the problem. What am I to do with them afterward?

You will remember that I warned you it would be next to impossible to extradite them. I urge you again to drop the investigation. We could not convict them if we did extradite them. I have $1,170 invested in four horses, $850 in the wagon, $320 in harness and saddle, $500 in tools, a total of $2,840 on top of prior expenses of $4,000 or more. To continue work here will cost at least $50 a day.

It is time to take your loss and drop it, rather than throw good money after bad. I don't like to waste anybody's money. This is a busy town. I can probably get $2,000 for the teams and outfit, cutting your loss that much. Think it over and wire me at the Devlin House. I remain, your most obedient servant,

Jefferson Hewitt

He sealed letter and picture in a hotel envelope, which he addressed to: *James W. Batchelder, Esq., Rafter B Cattle Co., Broken Bow, Nebr.* For safety's sake, he put the letter under his pillow.

He lay down, pulled the blanket over him, and decided upon one hour's sleep. He had trained himself to sleep anywhere, exactly as long as he wanted to sleep. His last waking thought was, Jim Batchelder will go up in flames when he sees that drawing. Quit now? I guess not! But my conscience is clear. I did my best to save his money . . .

CHAPTER TWO

Despite the noise in the street, Hewitt did not wake up until he had slept one hour. The rain had let up, but when he looked out of his window, he saw a dozen cowboys flailing away in a gang fight in the quagmire of the street. There was no sign of Ernie Hall, the town marshal the stableman had mentioned.

Hewitt shaved and put on clean clothing—black pants and frock coat, white shirt and tie, with the .32 under the shirt. He put the .45 under his coat, lighted a cigar, and went downstairs. It was almost ten o'clock, but when he went into the dining room, he had to wait half an hour for a table alone.

He ate a big meal, and a good one. He leaned back to enjoy the rest of his cigar with his coffee. A couple came into the dining room from the street door as Hewitt struck a match. He put the match out and stood up to bow as they passed his table.

"How do you do, Elsie?" he said. "You too, Devlin. It's easy to overlook you, but one mustn't."

"Do I know you?" Elsie Devlin said frowningly. "Say, I'll bet you're the fix-it man that talked that idiot of a Carrington into putting up your outfit."

"The same. You have prospered smartly since you left Omaha, my dear."

She paled slowly. "I—I don't know anybody named Hewitt."

"Everything changes, Elsie—even names."

"You're that damned Pinkerton man!" she cried suddenly.

Her pallor did not become her. At arm's length, she was less than the splendid creature she had appeared from a distance. Her magnificent red-blond hair had a metallic tint of chemicals. Her blue eyes were surrounded by fine wrinkles. Her stupendous bust had sagged.

"You're jumping to conclusions again, Elsie," he murmured.

"I am like hell! What did you call yourself there? It wasn't Hewitt! But you didn't fool me then, and you don't fool me now. What are you doing here?"

"Plying my trade. I'm merely a—"

"Oh, shut up that stuff!" She turned to her husband. "Paulie, you remember him, that damned Pinkerton flycop."

The handsome, flabby Devlin did not quite meet Hewitt's eyes. "What do we care?" he said. "Let him pry. Let him pry around all he likes!"

The woman recovered her poise. She said to Hewitt coldly, "You don't worry me. I inherited that money from the dearest friend I ever had in the world."

Hewitt raised one eyebrow. "All forty thousand dollars?"

"Five hundred dollars!"

"Did you start a saloon, a hotel, and a livery barn on five hundred dollars? That's good business, Elsie."

The waitress came to refill Hewitt's coffee cup. Mrs. Devlin waited until the girl had gone. "Listen, you! This is our town," she said rapidly, in a lower voice. "You start anything here, and you'll be sick of it faster than you think!"

"Let's not go behind the coroner's verdict," Hewitt said gently. "That fellow—what was his name?—oh, yes, Seth Johnson—committed suicide. The forty thousand dollars went up in smoke. Maybe the fairies got it. If your conscience is clear, my dear, that's all that counts."

"What are you doing in Dunsmuir?"

"I'm in clover, Elsie, and I'll take it ill if you spread tales that I'm a detective. I move with the seasons. No one tells me when to get up in the morning, or when to knock off for the day. There's many a cattleman has less cash at the end of the year than I. I have only one question I'd like to ask you."

"What?"

"Do you still have that wine-colored silk petticoat and the matching garters that I gave you?"

She threw up her head and walked on past to her corner table, her husband following without a glance at Hewitt. Out on the street, someone began shouting, "Train coming in—train coming in!" Most of the men in the dining room snatched up hats and oilskins, and made a dash for the door. Hewitt took his coffee and cigar to the window to watch.

It was a long freight, mostly slatted livestock cars, almost all of them full. The crew cut off twelve empties and backed into a side-track with them. More and more lanterns appeared at the loading chutes.

While he watched the scene at the tracks, Hewitt also watched the Devlins' reflection in the window. Elsie was definitely upset. She had more nerve than any woman he had never known. In a way, it was more than nerve. It was a headstrong vanity so towering that she simply did not believe a mere man could thwart her in anything.

But she was badly shaken now. Why?

The statute of limitations had outlawed any charge based on the theft of money. Elsie knew that as well as Hewitt did. But the statute never ran on murder. It could be prosecuted as long as the murderer lived.

Had the coroner been fooled about the death of Seth Johnson? Hewitt shook his head angrily at himself. He liked things neat and orderly. He had a job to do, and letting an old, unsolved case interfere now could ruin everything.

He put the Devlins out of his mind and sent old Bob, the bellboy, up to the room for his slicker and hat. He went down to the loading chutes with the letter to James W. Batchelder in his pocket. The rain had let up a little. In the light of a dozen lanterns, a mob was milling about the locomotive of the train. Hewitt stopped to watch and listen.

The conductor of the train stood in the cab of the engine, and behind him, the fireman held a double-barreled shotgun. "I got nothing to say about who gets the cars!" the conductor was shouting. "It's hard lines, gentlemen, but I can't help it, so don't take it out on us. Ain't no train going to stop here, ever, if you abuse the crews."

The cattlemen and their hands could have taken over the train—but what good would it have done them? They still depended on the railroad to move their cattle, whenever the railroad got around to it. They could and did call the conductor and the railroad foul names, but there would be no violence.

Hewitt walked along the train, ducking under the loading chutes. All the cattle being loaded wore the Fishhook brand. At one of the chutes, the chinless cowboy who called himself Tom Black was prodding steers up the chute with a pole. Hewitt spoke to another cowboy who was watching angrily from the dark.

"Excuse me, do you know that fellow up there?"

"Fishhook rider, that's all I know."

"Happen to know his sidekick?"

"No. Don't know anybody on the Fishhook, and don't want to."

"Who owns that outfit?"

"The Fishhook? Old Carl Hohn."

Hewitt asked him to spell it. He extracted all the information he could—and he was pretty good at extracting information. Hohn was one of the pioneers here, but he had few friends left among the other cattlemen. He was a money-maker, with the overbearing attitudes of so many of the rich. Only a certain kind of man could work for him.

Hewitt walked to the end of the train, where a surly brakeman leaned against the last car. He raised his lantern quickly to illuminate Hewitt's face. Hewitt handed him a cigar.

"Evening, boomer. Have a smoke on me."

The brakeman put the cigar in his shirt pocket. "Save it until we move out. You a railroader?"

"No more," Hewitt sighed. "I drop by now and then, to remind myself how lucky I am. But I've worked them all. The Central, the Pennsy, the Lehigh. The Illini, the Wabash, the Iron Mountain, the Nickel Plate. The Santa Fe, the U.P., the Denver & Rio Grande. Yes, I've boomed a bit, sir."

"I reckon I'll boom back and forth until I die. Too late to learn anything else."

"Like to ask a favor of you. Like you to mail that letter for me somewhere soon."

"There's a post office here."

Hewitt held up the letter and another five-dollar gold piece. "Don't want it seen here, you understand."

"I'll take care of it," the brakeman said.

Hewitt returned to the hotel, to get there ahead of the disgruntled cattlemen and their hands. He knew he could count on his letter being mailed. The floating railroaders who "boomed" the continent were a rough sort of fraternity who stuck together.

He stood a moment in front of the hotel, listening. Hewitt had a keen ear for crowd voices, and a cat's nerves for sensing a crowd's mood.

Carl Hohn and his Fishhook had had things their way for a long time, but this was the last year the neighbors would put up with this. Hewitt could tell whenever a Fishhook rider passed, by the hostile silence that fell until the man was out of hearing. He threw his cigar away and went inside.

"You fibbed to me, Mr. Hewitt," said the clerk. "You didn't see Mrs. Devlin before you came here."

"I didn't say I did. I merely said she'd tell you to give me a room. She did, didn't she?"

The clerk thought it over with a twisted grin. "Well, what she really said was, 'All right, but next time, don't be such a damned saphead sucker when a tinhorn detective runs a bluff on you.' Are you a Pinkerton?"

"No. That's one of Elsie's minor illusions."

"What are her major ones, Mr. Hewitt? You seem to know the lady better'n I do."

"I don't imagine she makes many mistakes. Have you got a Carl Hohn registered here?"

The clerk's affability vanished. "Look, you ask Mrs. Devlin if you want to know anything."

"Meaning that you have." Hewitt smiled. "So Carl Hohn is a special friend of Elsie's! No, you didn't say that, and I'll be the first to deny that you did. You and I understand each other, sir. Good night."

He went up the stairs slowly, his mind working rapidly. It was getting messy. The men he had come here to find worked for Carl Hohn. Hohn was a friend of Elsie Devlin, the only really successful female crook Hewitt had ever known. Maybe it was going to be impossible to keep things neat and tidy. Maybe the Devlins stood between him and Charley Kenyon and Slim Gurkey.

The more he thought about it, the deeper and more compelling became the warning sense that slid through him. Always before, it had paid him to heed these warnings. He would walk extra careful now.

He opened the door of number 12 silently, an inch at a

time. There was no one in the room; but again he made sure the blinds were drawn before lighting the lamps. Everything was exactly as he had left it, yet he knew the room and his suitcase had been thoroughly searched.

Hewitt smiled silently—let them search! Let them search his house wagon, too, as no doubt they had. The more they searched, the less they would find.

It was raining again when he went to bed, with his .45 under his pillow and a chair propped under the doorknob. He slept well. The bed was sheer luxury, after so many nights in his musty wagon bunk.

Jefferson Hewitt's conscience might have been the cleanest one in town.

He was—or had been—a Pinkerton operative because he liked the money it paid, and did not mind being despised by his fellow men. "Jefferson Hewitt" was not his real name. He had been born to the name of Hugh Goff, but he had also been known, over the years, as Aaron B. London, Zeke Harvey, Alec Laidlaw, Richard Bing, W. A. Chastain, and Reuben Whitman.

He had used some of these names several times, changing character and personality to go with them. It had never bothered him to lay aside his soul thus. He had no home town, no family, no roots, no human ties anywhere.

Born in the Missouri Ozarks, he had joined the Army at age fifteen. He was twenty when the riots occurred at the Presidio of San Francisco, where he was a corporal and the company clerk. That is, they were riots on the records. The word, mutiny, was never committed to paper.

But mutiny was what the men had in mind. Corporal

Goff arranged to be across the bay, in Oakland, on official business, when whatever it was exploded. Whatever it was, it was put down in two days. On the third day, the commanding general had Corporal Goff in for one of those man-to-man talks so dreaded by enlisted men, who always emerge losers.

"When I want the truth, I go to a good noncom," the general said. "On my word of honor that you'll never be connected with it, I want to know what happened. Now, let's drop the 'sir' and be friends. You talk like an educated man, I'm told."

"Self-educated." He carefully omitted "sir."

"Why?"

"I don't like to be at a disadvantage, and I was pretty ignorant when I joined up."

That fit what the general had been told. "All right, Corporal—what made the men go berserk?"

"They wanted to kill the captain—and to anticipate your next question, he had it coming. He's a drunk, a bully, a thief, and a seducer of enlisted men's wives, sweethearts, and daughters."

"I suppose you can prove that."

"*You* can. Why would I bother to prove it? The captain is nothing to me."

The general drummed on the desk a moment. "I'm told that you run the company, yet you don't appear to be one of the captain's pets, Corporal."

"I'm not. Somebody has to do the work. Doing it gives me safety and stature. The lieutenants aren't much good, and they're demoralized because the captain ignores them and works through the sergeants. The fool thinks they enjoy fraternizing with him, but they hate him worse than anyone. I'd work on them, General. The company needs new officers, but the sergeants are good men."

"I think that will be all, Corporal Goff," the general said.

"Yes sir," Corporal Goff said. He saluted before he left the room.

The company—with the exception of Corporal Goff—was confined to quarters for a week. The lieutenants were transferred. The captain was permitted to resign. Long before the new officers arrived, Corporal Goff's term of enlistment had expired.

He did not sign over, having been offered a job with the Pinkertons. Obviously, the general had a hand in that. It was both an expression of gratitude and a way of getting rid of an obnoxious noncom.

The job paid more than a boy from the Ozarks had a right to expect. He remained with the Pinkertons for five years. He liked the work. He liked the adventure of out-witting—or perhaps outshooting—a thief, spy, or home-wrecker. He was especially good on divorce and/or seduction cases, being young, presentable, and in complete control of his emotions.

He was still better on cases involving stolen horses and cattle, because of his rural background. He became so good at this, in fact, that a Wyoming bank offered to set him up in business.

Hewitt now worked out of his own office in Cheyenne. He had a partner, Conrad Meuse. The name of the firm was Bankers' Bonding and Indemnity Company. Meuse, a fanatically honest but unimaginative German immigrant, took care of the bonding of clerks, treasurers, salesmen, and commission men. Hewitt ran the investigative end of the business.

He still enjoyed the work and the money he made, and it still did not bother him that people despised him when he was unmasked at an arrest or trial. He lived in the best hotels, when he could, and ate the best food, and wore the finest clothing. But he could let his whiskers grow and do a cowboy's work with the old hands, when he had to.

Now, at thirty-six, he did not know what he wanted out of life, but not knowing caused him no anguish. He liked physical comfort, but to get a job done, he could be uncomfortable as long as he took.

He liked women, but was not a slave to them.

He drank sparingly of good aged whiskies and fine wines, but had never been drunk.

He avoided danger without dodging it.

As a rule, he was dedicated to justice, and had quit a few cases because he thought B.B. & I.C. had been retained by the wrong side. But he was not a crusader.

He went to church when the job called for it, but he was not religious. At the same time, a prodigious memory had given him a fund of Bible quotations that more than once had come in handy.

He was a good horseman, a good cook, an artist of professional skill, a better-than-average mechanic and carpenter, and an excellent masseur. He had learned this art from a physician he was investigating for embezzlement, and whom he later convicted.

He was an excellent shot, with long or short gun.

He spoke English with a dozen accents, depending on the job. He spoke bad Spanish fluently, had a fair command of German—enough to irritate his partner, Conrad Meuse, who said that Hewitt talked like a *gottverdammt Osterreicher*. He could get by in French.

He was a fair boxer, but at only 159 lbs., he did not go about looking for fist-fights. He could handle a knife, although he did not carry one. In his suitcase he carried a shot-filled leather sap, with which he had a surgeon's precision and skill.

Most of the time, Jefferson Hewitt slept with a conscience as clear as a baby's. He so slept tonight.

CHAPTER THREE

He came awake as he hit the floor. He hit it in total silence, the gun from under his pillow already in his hand. Two men were arguing in the hallway just outside his door, and only one was trying to keep his voice down.

"Aw, come on! She ain't in there, you danged fool!" That would be the chinless one, Charley Kenyon, *alias* Tom Black. Hewitt already knew that voice.

"She is too! God durn her, she lied to me!" the other said loudly, a sob in his voice. "Mandy! You hear me, Mandy? You come out of there before I come in!"

"Hell with you. You ain't getting me in trouble," said Tom Black.

His boots clumped rapidly down the stairs. Hewitt rolled over and came up on his belly and elbows in his underwear. He could hear the other man just outside the door, breathing so hard he was almost weeping.

"Mandy. What you trying to do to me, Mandy? I'm going to kill me, you two-timing me in there, Mandy!"

Hewitt wriggled backward, out of the line of fire between doorway and bed. He propped himself up on his left elbow, and thumbed back the hammer of the .45.

He thought he knew when a man was only pretending to be drunk. This one was not pretending. Slim Gurkey,

Charley Kenyon's partner? Probably. Had someone put him up to this? Was Hewitt supposed to fling the door open indignantly, and get shot over a woman who was not in his room?

"Mandy, I'm going to count to three, and then I'm comin' in. One . . . Two . . . *Three!*"

The first shot splintered the lock, but when the drunken man in the hall tried the knob, it still held. The next shot blew what was left of the lock off the door, and took part of the door frame with it. Someone began screaming in a room down the hall.

It was a woman, and the screams stopped suddenly, as though a hand had been clamped over her mouth. The door slammed back, and a man stumbled into the room. His silhouette was short and chunky, and not steady on its feet.

At the bedside, the drunk leaned over and rubbed his face with his left hand. He was mumbling loudly, half choked by sobs. Hewitt took careful aim, but he let the drunk fire once into the empty bed before he pulled his own trigger.

He knew that he had hit the man in the bone of the upper arm. You never forgot the sound of a bullet in bone, once you heard it. And you never underestimated the paralyzing shock of a bad bone wound again, either.

The drunk man made no sound. He twisted as he collapsed to the floor, and lay inertly. Hewitt came to his feet and crossed the room in two steps. He pushed the unconscious man's gun aside with his bare foot. He could hear someone in the hall.

"Get a light in here, and call the law!" he shouted. "I had to shoot some poor fool that shot his way in."

Old Bob Kramer ran up from the lobby, a gun in one hand and a lamp in the other. Hewitt turned the wounded man over. He was unconscious, and in the pale lamplight looked ghastly. Dark, good-looking face gone bluish-pale from shock, under a heavy growth of black whiskers. Heavy, unkempt shock of dark, curly brown hair.

Not as heavy as he had looked in silhouette; under his mackinaw coat, he was slim and wiry. A description that would fit a hundred men in Dunsmuir tonight, no doubt. It also fit Slim Gurkey, quite accurately.

"Is he dead?" Kramer said.

"No. Where's your town marshal?" Hewitt replied.

"I sent for him. He's prob'ly asleep, but he'll get here soon."

"Is there a doctor in town? I don't want this poor fool to lose that arm, if it can be saved."

A tall, broad-shouldered old man with gray whiskers pushed through the crowd, pulling his suspenders up over his bare shoulders. He looked like the kind of old man who was used to having people get out of his way; and they did. He came into the room on his knobby old bare feet.

"A man pays for a night's sleep," he said in a harsh, bullying voice. "What's going on in this hotel?"

"Sorry, Carl, but this fool busted into Mr. Hewitt's room and got hisself shot," old Bob Kramer said. "He's one of your boys, ain't he?"

Carl Hohn leaned over to look. "Why, this is Bill Anderson. Look at the way that arm is bent! He'll lose that arm. Who shot him?"

Hewitt put his .45 on a chair while he stepped into his

own pants. "I did," he said. "I take it that you're Carl Hohn."

"What'd you shoot him fer?"

"Look at that door!" Hewitt shouted. "Are you deaf as well as stupid, old man? He was looking for somebody called Mandy. He shot the lock out of the door, and he shot into my bed just before I fired at him."

The two men faced each other. Old Hohn towered over Hewitt. "I can't hardly believe Bill Anderson would shoot up the hotel," Hohn said. "Why would he do that?"

"I told you! A woman called Mandy."

"That's mighty loose talk. I didn't hear nobody say nothing like that! You're so free with your gun—"

Hewitt cut in, "Wait a minute! Tell you what let's do. Let's go through these rooms one at a time, until we find somebody by the name of Mandy. He came to the wrong room, is all. Which is the right room?"

The wounded man began to whimper. It seemed to Hewitt that old Hohn was glad to change the subject. He knelt beside Bill Anderson. "Poor boy, first time I ever seen him drunk, and it'll cost him an arm," he said. "Let me get dressed, and somebody go get the doctor."

Ernie Hall, the town marshal, came up the stairs. Hewitt liked him instantly. Hall asked what questions he had to ask, and he seemed to be able to listen to several people at once. Others had heard the drunken cowboy yelling for Mandy. All told the same story that Hewitt had told—all but old Hohn.

By the old man's eagerness to get back to his room and get dressed, Hewitt had no trouble guessing where the missing Mandy was. He thought that others in the hotel had the same hunch.

The wounded man was carried down the stairs, weeping in agony. Marshal Hall, a plain-looking, middle-aged man in a business suit, ordered everyone out of Hewitt's room. He closed the door, while Hewitt lighted both lamps.

"Elsie will have to replace the door as well as the lock, I'm afraid," Hewitt said.

"You're the Pinkerton man," Hall said.

"I'm not a Pinkerton man. I'm a journeyman repairman. My outfit is at the livery stable."

"I know! The party who told me that you're a Pinkerton is generally right."

Hewitt smiled. "Right she usually is! But she's wrong this time. It shouldn't take much of a search to find someone called Mandy, who could clear this shooting up. Do you know her?"

"I know who she is."

"How long would it take me to prove that she works for the Royal? For the Devlins."

Hall said, "What I wonder is who told Bill she'd be in your room."

"A good question, Marshal."

"Got any good answers? Another good one—why is Mrs. Devlin so upset because there's a detective in town?"

The more I see of this small-town officer, the more I like him, Hewitt thought . . . He said, "As the Scots say, women are kittle cattle. Who knows why Elsie thinks or does or says anything?"

Hall seemed to make up his mind. He dropped his voice.

"Mr. Hewitt, my wife and me have got a little grocery store here. Keeping the peace here is a part-time job, except when they're shipping cattle. I used to get some help from the cattlemen. Not any more. They just don't care any more."

"Especially Carl Hohn."

"Well, yes. Carl used to be a steady sort of man. Been married to a good woman for upwards of forty years. Now look what's got into him!"

"When did it get into him? How long has he been making a nuisance of himself?"

"Couple of years. No fool like an old fool—"

"How long have the Devlins been here?"

"Upwards of four years. Yes, they're friends with Carl. What are you driving at?"

"Marshal, how much cash could Hohn raise?"

"Carl's in debt up to his ears! Didn't used to be. He don't know that I know that he put a second mortgage on his place a while back."

"For how much?"

"Twelve thousand is what I hear."

"And took it in cash?"

"I don't know."

"Can you find out?"

"Maybe. Why should I?"

"Don't, then. You're the law here."

Hall frowned. "Mr. Hewitt, you cause me to think, yes you do! When I heared there was a Pinkerton in town, I made up my mind to ask him help me keep the peace. Now I'm purely determined to have you!"

"You're offering me a job as your deputy?"

"Yes. It'll only pay a dollar and a quarter a night, and it's nights I need you. Mostly it'd be just keeping the peace in the saloons."

"I'm not a Pinkerton, Marshal Hall," Hewitt said smilingly, "but I don't mind helping out. One objection occurs to me. The Royal—do I keep the peace there, too?"

"Yes. Devlin is the first to holler for help when the boys get to fighting and breaking up his things. Rest of the time, he don't want to see you around. I'm a businessman myself. I know how he feels," Hall said.

"But there've been two men killed in the Royal in the last couple of years, and a couple found dead in the street that the gossip was, they was shot in the Royal and dragged outside to die. They get them poor ignorant riders in there, and take their money away from them, and you can't blame them for wanting to fight when they wake up and see how they've been deadfalled.

"I don't like that way of doing business, Mr. Hewitt. Keep the peace in the Royal too, by all means! Would it do any good to ask you where and when you knowed the Devlins before they came here?"

Hewitt shook his head. The officer did not take offense. When Hall left, Jefferson Hewitt was a deputy marshal of Dunsmuir, Kansas. He went to the head of the stairs and whistled softly for Bob Kramer.

"Get me a pot of black coffee, Mr. Kramer, can you? I've got some thinking to do before I sleep again."

Hewitt had been on the Batchelder case for a year and a half, the longest he had ever worked a case. So far, not a cent had been paid on the fee, but Batchelder had shelled out generously for expenses.

Jim Batchelder was about sixty, a hard-driving, ignorant but money-making man who had amassed a fortune in land and cattle near Broken Bow, Nebraska. Some forty miles away lived his younger brother, Ed Batchelder, and Ed's common-law wife.

Jim and Ed had never been close, and in the last few years there had been real hostility between them. No one knew what had caused it except the brothers themselves, and they refused to talk. Jim would not go into this part of it, either, when Jefferson Hewitt took the case.

One hot and humid morning, Ed Batchelder saddled a horse and told his "wife," Edna, that he had a meeting with his brother. He owed Jim some money, but the woman did not know if they were to meet about that. "Jim and me is going to straighten a few things out, once and for all," was her recollection of his last words as he went out the door.

He did not come home. His body was found the next morning, on Rafter B range. Ed had been shot four times in the chest. Any one of the wounds would have caused instantaneous death. His gun—unfired—lay a few feet from the body. The evidence showed that he had got it out, but had been dead before he could squeeze off a shot.

Could one man have fired four times, fast enough to hit Ed before he dropped? The Sheriff of Custer County thought not. Had two or more men forced him to draw, and then shot him in a volley? This sounded more likely. Ed's pockets had been emptied, and his horse was missing.

The country was full of job-hunting drifters. Suspicion fell on two men who had worked for Jim Batchelder, Charley Kenyon and Slim Gurkey, both about twenty. They had arrived in Custer County together, and had quit their jobs a few days before the murder.

Ed had died without leaving a will. His common-law marriage was invalid for testamentary purposes. His "widow" would get nothing, and his brother, Jim, would get everything Ed had owned—unless it could be proved that Jim was guiltily responsible for the murder.

The probate was put "off calendar," while the sheriff tried to unravel the case. On his bank's advice, Jim called in Bankers' Bonding and Indemnity Company. "I don't care about the property," Jim told Jefferson Hewitt, in their first interview. "I just want to find who killed Ed."

It was an old murder by then, the trails gone stale. "It'll be hard to find those two cowboys, Mr. Batchelder," Hewitt said. "Not much chance of proving it on them if I do find them. I don't think you have any idea how much an investigation will cost.

"When the bills start coming in for it, sir, after the tears have dried, it usually happens that the need to convict somebody suddenly becomes less urgent. I think you're perfectly sincere—*now*. But the bills and the passage of time somehow bring about a loss of heart."

Jim growled, "Not with me! I've got some money in the bank, and I'm going to cash in some railroad bonds. I can raise close to thirty thousand. You should be able to wind it up for that. If you can't—well, let me know when thirty thousand is about gone, and I'll see how much I can raise by mortgaging the Rafter B."

"Suppose I find them, and they tell me that you paid them to kill your brother?"

"That'll be the biggest lie ever told. Bring them back here and let the sheriff get the truth out of them."

The sheriff had his doubts too. "Kenyon and Gurkey are innocent until proved guilty," he told Hewitt. "I'm looking for them because they're likely suspects, but you know the doctrine of reasonable doubt, don't you?"

"I know the doctrine of reasonable doubt."

"All we've got is circumstantial evidence, and no jury likes to convict on that, in a hanging case. So if you aim to bring back Kenyon and Gurkey, and then expect me to earn your fee for you—"

"You look here! I was hired to clear up this murder. I'm starting with Kenyon and Gurkey for the same reason you are—they're the best suspects. If I find that they didn't do it, I'll look elsewhere. If I prove that Jim Batchelder killed his brother, I'll consider my job done and demand my fee."

"I dunno if I'd want you investigating a case of mine, Mr. Hewitt."

"I don't care who did it, just so I find that right man. Be seeing you, Sheriff."

Kenyon and Gurkey both came from Indiana. They had punched cows all over the entire West—from Alberta to Sonora and back. As Hewitt groped their dim backtrail, he began to find the pattern he sought. Whenever they went broke, the two headed for Kansas City, Missouri. There they roomed near the railroad yards, where they could always pick up a little work on the track gang. When they had a few dollars in their pockets, they moved on.

After he realized that they would never get far from Kansas City, Hewitt quickly picked up their trail—McCook, Grand Island, Nebraska City, Falls City, Kansas City, Abilene, Topeka, Dodge City, Wichita. Hewitt rode the trains in a boomer's clothes and a week's growth of beard.

He never caught up with Kenyon and Gurkey, but he figured out how to entrap them. It would cost money, however. Back to Broken Bow he went, to see how Jim Batchelder felt after all these months and all these thousands of dollars.

Jim felt just fine. "I feel better, knowing you're on their heels, Mr. Hewitt. I know you're going to find the men that killed my brother," he said.

"That's more than I know," said Hewitt.

"You'll search them out, and I don't care how much money it costs. Half the people around here think I killed my own brother. Find them, Mr. Hewitt. Find the truth!"

It took a month to get the house wagon built and to find the horses Hewitt wanted, in St. Joe. It took two more weeks to finish outfitting the wagon.

Now, for a year, he had been Mr. Fix-It. He had never doubted that he would find Kenyon and Gurkey. Long ago, he had become convinced of their guilt. They kept moving like guilty men, each afraid to let the other out of his sight. He was always ready to pounce.

Now the time to pounce had come.

And just as he poised to pounce, up popped the Devlin-Cushman case, which he had never expected to hear of again. Gertrude Cushman was an aged widow who owned a lot of good Omaha property. She was old enough to be a bit foolish, but she was believed to be sharp as a tack about business and money matters.

Gertrude Cushman was kicked to death by her own buggy team, in sight of a dozen witnesses. There was no possibility of foul play—but when her will was read, the case became news overnight. There were two small bequests, $500 each to Seth Johnson, the handyman who took care of her horses, and Elsie Ogilvie, who ran a workingmen's hotel in a property leased from Mrs. Cushman.

The balance, estimated to be close to $50,000, went to the Methodist Church. When the court-appointed executor dug into things, he found that the estate had melted away to little more than $3,000. Every piece of property the old woman had owned had been mortgaged to the hilt.

The loans came from five different banks. No one bank had any reason to be suspicious. The strange thing about all these loans was that the proceeds had been taken *in cash*. Many an eccentric old woman liked to deal in cash. But $40,000 of it? And from five different banks?

The local pastor of the Methodist Church retained Bankers' Bonding and Indemnity Company to investigate. On this case, Hewitt was Aaron B. London, buyer for an Albany, New York, horse broker. His first act was to make friends with Seth Johnson, a solitary, short-tempered man whose only interest in life was horses. He drank more than was good for him. The $500 he inherited from Mrs. Cushman did not last long.

Among horsemen, there was a lodge-brother spirit like that among boomers. Many a night, Aaron B. London and Seth Johnson sat in a stable somewhere, drinking and talking about horses.

Incredible though it seemed at first, it dawned on London that old Seth was wildly, hopelessly in love with Elsie

Ogilvie. The day that Elsie suddenly married a bartender, Paul Devlin, Seth either jumped or was pushed off the roof of a four-story building.

He landed head first on a brick sidewalk, and never uttered another word. The Methodist preacher—a good man that Aaron B. London liked and respected—called off the investigation. The church, he said, did not want to profit from any more deaths . . .

You win about four hands, Jefferson Hewitt told himself, along about daylight, and then you lose one. The skill of poker consisted in losing the little pots and winning the big ones. He had a rich and profitable client in Jim Batchelder. Could he afford to be distracted by the memory of the missing $40,000 of the Cushman estate?

He had never had much doubt about where the money had gone. He thought that Seth Johnson had suspected it too, and had killed himself rather than face the truth about the woman he adored so hopelessly. When she married weak, pompous, and foolish Paul Devlin, it was the last straw for the mixed-up old man.

Now, Hewitt thought, where do I go from here? My two cases are all tangled up. Nothing to be made from the Cushman case, unless I can recover some of the missing money. No question, Elsie is richer than she has any business being. But how prove it's Cushman money . . . ?

And how did Elsie now figure in the Batchelder murder? Every instinct in the manhunter told him that she was in it up to her lovely, if now somewhat sagging, neck. The thing to do, of course, was put the Cushman case aside, until he had solved the Batchelder case.

But could that be done?

Hewitt had disciplined himself to the rule that first things came first. It would only confuse him, to start speculating about either case now. His job was to find the murderers of Ed Batchelder. If the Cushman case popped up and demanded attention during the course of that job—well, time enough to face it when it happened.

At daylight, he put the whole mess out of his mind. He cleaned his gun, as he did after every firing, because that was the next logical thing to do. The simple act of cleaning it eased his mind and reassured him of the logic of his methods. First things first, always.

CHAPTER FOUR

There was a nip of frost in the air when Hewitt awakened at eight o'clock. As he walked to the livery stable after breakfast in the hotel, he heard only two topics of conversation among the restless men milling about on the sidewalks.

The first was himself. They had him identified as the Pinkerton trick shot who had winged Bill Anderson last night. They made way for him, but there was not a friendly face in the crowd.

The other was the rumor that a train with a hundred empties would arrive early this afternoon. Most of these riders were broke now. They would soon head south to a warmer climate, and the dollar a day they would make until the cattle were loaded was not very tempting. They were as sick of Dunsmuir as Dunsmuir was of them.

Hewitt went into the barn. He could hear the stableman, George Carrington, talking to someone in the far corner of the barn.

"I don't know why you're so p'tic'lar now, Carl," he was saying. "Shape these horses was in when you brought them here, you'd think some gypsy owned them. They sure hadn't been combed and brushed yestiddy, by gadsy!"

"My back was out," came Carl Hohn's surly growl.

"It's killin' me this morning. I been waking up every day with a backache. If it wasn't for this pain, you couldn't handle a horse of mine!"

Hewitt walked through the barn to the box stall next to his own teams, where Carrington was harnessing a team for Carl Hohn. The old rancher had himself propped up on a stick, his bearded face twisted with suffering.

"Ah there, Mr. Hohn! How's the man I had to wing last night?" Hewitt said affably.

Hohn turned his back on Hewitt without answering. Over a horse's back, Carrington winked at Hewitt. "Morning, Mr. Hewitt," he said. "Your team has already been fed."

"Good! I'll want to set up shop this morning. Now that the rain has let up a little, I expect to do a nice little turn of business."

The old cattleman could stand it no longer. He turned painfully, leaning on his stick. "Why don't you jist push right on out of town, Pinkerton man?" he said. "Your kind ain't wanted here."

"I'm not a Pinkerton man," Hewitt replied, with a smile, "and I like your town too much to leave it. I regret very much having had to shoot that idiot last night. I asked you once how he is. I'm asking you again."

"Too early to tell. Doc Hanrahan is going to try to save that arm, if he can."

"I sincerely hope he can."

"I bet you do! You deliberately drilled him right through the bone."

"Damn it, he came into a dark room, firing his gun. I

didn't care where I hit him, man! Anyplace to drop him, before he killed me."

"What I hear, Pinkerton man, is that what you shoot at, you hit. You're a circus gunman, I hear."

"Mr. Hohn, when you know Elsie Devlin as well as I do, you'll trim off a lot of waste and fat from everything she says. There is no need for us to quarrel, Mr. Hohn. To prove my goodwill, I'd like to relieve your aching back. I can do it with scientific pressure and massage, and the whole world will look brighter when that pain is gone."

"I'd sooner let a rattlesnake touch me. Sooner you leave wheel tracks leading out of this town, the better suited we'll be here."

"It's your back. Go ahead and suffer! It must make you look rather ridiculous to Mandy, however."

Hohn's eyes glittered at him furiously, but he said nothing. Carrington led the team out and harnessed them to a handsome top-buggy. He had to help Hohn into the buggy and hand him the lines. Hewitt remained in the stable until the buggy had disappeared.

"Listen, Mr. Hewitt—what did you mean when you said that about Mandy?" Carrington wanted to know, when he came back into the stable.

"How long has Hohn been chasing after women?" Hewitt countered.

"Him? I never heard of him looking at another woman. He's got a mighty sweet old wife. Did you mean he's chasing who I think you meant?"

Again Hewitt deflected the question. "What do you know about this kid I had to shoot last night?"

"Bill Anderson? Not much. No real meanness in Bill, but you can't say that about his partner. That Tom Black, he's another proposition."

"What do you know about Bill's lady friend?"

"Didn't know he had one until today. Kind of surprised me, when they said he was trying to smoke some woman out when he shot his way into your room. Who was she?"

"Somebody he called Mandy. Probably her real name is Amanda."

"Amanda Rody?" Carrington cried. "That pore kid must be plumb out of his mind! Amanda helps Mrs. Devlin with the books, and writes her letters for her. She ain't no saloon hustler! If Bill Anderson was fooling around with her, he'll have Mrs. Devlin down on him like a ton of bricks! Where was she during the shootin' last night?"

"I have no idea," Hewitt said, not quite truthfully. I think I'm beginning to catch on, he thought. She was with Carl Hohn. Why? Money, of course. Oh Elsie, Elsie, aren't you a cute one . . .

It would be like Elsie to import some attractive, unscrupulous girl, and keep her looking demure and chaste and unavailable, to drive an old fool like Carl Hohn crazy. Also, it would be exactly like such a nitwit girl to fall for a worthless cowboy like Slim Gurkey, *alias* Bill Anderson. And try to double-cross everybody—the cowboy, Carl Hohn and, most dangerous of all, Elsie Devlin.

He would have to have a look at Amanda Rody. Meanwhile, first things first. Another ten-dollar gold piece to Carrington provided him with a place to set up his shop. In good weather, Hewitt's fix-it business required no shelter.

He set up wherever he liked, protecting himself and his tools against an occasional shower by stretching a tarp behind his wagon.

In this sea of mud, in a wet fall, he needed better shelter. He backed his wagon in against a ramshackle roof used to shelter wagons and buggies, only one of which had to be moved to make room. He found a sawn log of firewood length on which to mount his little anvil, and a shorter one for a seat.

He set up his little forge under the roof, and laid his tools out on top of the tool chest. He hung up his oilcloth signs, and then went around town to put out his handbills, filling in their blank spaces with crayon. They repeated the message painted on the sides of his wagon.

He made his first call at the blacksmith shop. "I'm a repairman myself, and I got no use for detectives," the smith said gruffly. "Don't hang no bills up in here."

"I'm not a detective, and I won't take any trade from you. Anything a blacksmith should do, I'll send them to you."

"That's what you tell me, anyway."

"My friend, you can't break even plugging holes in milk buckets, soldering tincups and teakettles, and brazing the clips of a clock spring! Do you patch saddles, grind scissors, and replace corset staves? That's my line of work!"

He made a friend of the blacksmith quickly. "I feel sorry for that kid if he loses an arm," the smith said, "but I reckon he asked fer it. I don't know him, but his sidekick can't even come into my shop."

"Tom Black? Why?"

"I seen him beat a horse with an endgate rod until they

took it away from him. Then I thought he was going to kill them for doing it. I'd watch him if I was you, sir."

"I'm not afraid of small-town horse-beaters."

"You better be afraid of this one! I think Tom Black is going to die, and he knows it and is afraid to die."

"Of what?"

"Consumption! They say he coughs up blood. He don't drink or run after women. All he does is gamble, and he don't get no fun out of that, even. I think what's in the back of his mind is to work himself up to a gunfight, where he can cut his own misery short and maybe take somebody with him. You watch out for him, mister!"

Hewitt thanked him and walked on with his handbills, thinking soberly. What the blacksmith had said reminded him of the kind of man who could have killed Ed Batchelder in cold blood. The very viciousness of that four-shot killing had been the one puzzling thing. Now he thought he could see the kind of gunfighter who could kill that way.

A few of these half-mad gunmen removed the triggers, or at least filed down the tangs, of their guns. They then fanned the hammer, striking it with palm or the heel of the other hand, instead of pulling the trigger. It wasn't as accurate as shooting with the trigger, but oh, it was fast! At a short distance, it was a form of execution, not a gunfight.

Had Charley Kenyon, *alias* Tom Black, learned to fan a triggerless gun? That would fill in another blank space in the puzzle. One man would have the answer, and he lay somewhere with his left arm shattered, while another man decided whether or not to cut it off.

But first things first.

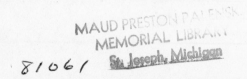

Hewitt did a thriving business that day. They were waiting for him when he got back to the livery stable after putting out his handbills. He had trouble finding time to go to the hotel for lunch.

His customers this day were the respectable housewives of Dunsmuir, who did not venture out on the main street of their own town while the cattlemen were shipping. They reached the livery barn by a series of back paths, and how glad they were to get out of the house! They brought their leaking pots and pans, their broken clocks and watches, churns and scissors, knives and cheap jewelry.

Hewitt had a way with women, especially those he labeled as "good" in his own mind. He was not just respectful—he was elaborately courteous, almost courtly.

"Yes, ma'am, I can fix that. Can do it while you wait, ma'am, if you're in a hurry, and delighted to do so."

They wanted to wait. He kept his place and let them carry the conversation. When he replied, he used the folksy speech of the frontier, and his softest voice.

"You've seen a lot of towns, Mr. Hewitt."

"Surely I have, ma'am. One after another."

"What do you think of our town?"

"Why . . . it has the makings of a nice town, ma'am."

"The makings? Don't you like it now?"

"Excuse me, ma'am, but it's still pretty rough. It's a man's town, not a family town, see? That will change. Someday it will be a good place to bring up kids."

"I see. You're right! Now that the kids are getting bigger, I dread shipping time. You just can't keep them off the street or away from the tracks. I—I heard you had to shoot a man last night, Mr. Hewitt. That's just awful!"

"Yes, ma'am. Here you are, good as new. Twenty-five cents, ma'am, and thank you for your custom."

He learned a lot about Dunsmuir. He had always known that Western men underestimated the power of their women. Usually, the Western woman kept her place.

But push her too far, and a man armed only with a gun came out loser. Hewitt knew, before the day was over, that in any collision between himself and Elsie Devlin, he would have the women of Dunsmuir on his side.

When it came time to put the potatoes on to fry, the women stopped coming and the cowboys drifted in. Most were broke, or close to it. They had spent their dollars at the Royal, and now must hoard their dimes.

Mostly they just wanted to talk to someone. Hewitt changed personalities with them. He became precise in his grammar, and a little scholarly in his choice of words. He talked so softly that they had to strain to listen. A man concentrating on listening, he had found, was usually a little careless in his talk.

"You're the Pinkerton man that shot Bill Anderson, ain't you?"

"I am not a Pinkerton man."

"You shot it out with Bill, though."

"We had a little trouble, yes."

"I'd like to know just what did happen."

"I never talk about a man behind his back, sir. They say he may lose his arm. I regret that very much."

"It wouldn't lose me no sleep! That son of a bitch he runs with, that Tom Black—he's a killer."

"Nonsense! Many a chap has been ruined by a small-town reputation he doesn't deserve. I don't mean to have trouble with Mr. Black."

"Mister, ha! I'll give you some advice, and I don't care if you are a Pinkerton. If Tom comes after you, don't try to wing him. Shoot to kill!"

At this point, Hewitt laid down his tools and looked his man in the eye. "My friend, I'm too old a horned toad to be talked into a shoot-out with a tank-town badman. I'll thank you not to retail that kind of talk around town."

That man, hurrying off with his mended spur jingling, or a new buckle on his belt, could not wait to pass on the word. "That Pinkerton man is a cold-blooded son! Called Tom Black a tank-town badman. That's just daring Black to go after him, and I'd bet even money either way on that fight."

It was sundown, and Hewitt was closing up his shop. A middle-aged cowboy, far gone in liquor, came reeling through the mud.

"Sorry, my friend. I'm through for the day."

"Aw, shoot! I wanted a portrait. How much do you charge for a portrait?"

"Of whom?"

"Of me. Who the hell do you think?"

"It's too dark for portraiture, my friend. Better wait until tomorrow."

"May not be alive tomorrow. You can draw me by lantern light, can't you?"

"Yes, I suppose so," Hewitt said amusedly, "but what makes you think you may not be alive tomorrow?"

The cowboy began to weep. "I had three hundred dollars coming when we bedded the herd down here. I got six dollars left. I want the biggest pitcher of me you can draw for that."

"What will you do with it?"

"Make a present to the Royal. The Sioux claim that your spirit follers your likeness. They got everything else of mine—the Royal might as well have my soul, too."

Hewitt laughed. He got out two lanterns and lighted them. He seated the cowboy on the back steps of the wagon and began to draw his picture with swift, sure strokes.

"You work for the Fishhook?"

"Used to. Not no more! That's a riffraff outfit."

"Did you know Bill Anderson?"

"Him that got his arm shot off? No, but I've met his sidekick, Tom Black. That's all I want of him."

"Anderson's arm wasn't shot off."

"It was cut off this afternoon. Doc sawed it off about three inches from the shoulder."

"I'm so sorry to hear that!"

"You'll be sorrier, if Tom Black comes after you."

"Nonsense! Where is Anderson? I might go see him and assure him I meant him no harm."

"He's at Doc Hanrahan's house. Big yella two-story house, biggest in town. You cain't miss it. The upstairs two bedrooms is his hospital. Last I heard, Bill Anderson was still sleepin' off the chloroform."

"I wonder what he'll do now?"

"I hear that there's going to be a flour mill in town, and Carl Hohn promised a job there to Bill."

"A flour mill?"

"Yes. It's going to wheat real fast around here. They say

everybody with any money is tryin' to get in on the flour mill, but they won't take in everybody."

"I see." Hewitt finished the portrait. "There, how does it look to you?"

"Just like it's supposed to look—the saddest fool that ever busted twenty-one six times in a row," the cowboy said, with maudlin gravity. "I'm going to give it to Mother Devlin to hang just inside the front door, so the hull nation can laugh at the fool I be."

Hewitt burst out laughing. "Is that what they call her —Mother Devlin?"

"Well, not to her face. How much do I owe you?"

"Put your money away. Suppose we inscribe a little verse under the picture—" Hewitt scribbled a moment on a piece of paper, and then read off what he had written. "How does that sound to you?"

"Fine! Kin you put that poem under the pitcher?"

"Surely! Then you hang it in the Royal, and the portrait will cost you nothing."

In heavy black letters, in a purple framework draped with black, Hewitt printed:

FAREWELL TO MOTHER DEVLIN

When the last poor puncher is busted,
*   And she stops for a moment of prayer,*
Somebody tell Mother Devlin
*   This cowboy won't be there.*
I've drunk of her rotgut whiskey,
*   And I've played her crooked games,*
But if ever I see her again, it'll be
*   In hell's own hottest flames.*

The cowboy hurried unsteadily toward town, with the picture rolled up in his hand. Ah Elsie, Hewitt thought, the one thing a person in your position can't stand is ridicule. Now it's a flour mill, is it? With everyone laughing . . . ?

A train whistled into town as he strolled toward the hotel for supper. Every man in town raced through the mud to meet it. Hewitt counted thirty cars in the string of empties that the crew set out. Hewitt did not cross the street to the train, but he remained a moment to watch and listen. The Fishhook got twenty of the cars, but the train crew brought the rumor that empties were being collected for an extra train tomorrow—at least eighty cars.

At the Royal, the bartender was in the doorway, watching the excitement at the tracks. "Is Mrs. Devlin in?" Hewitt asked him.

"No, sir, she sure ain't."

"Can you tell me where I might find her?"

"I maybe could, but I won't."

Hewitt had no desire to have trouble with the bartender, and no need to know where Elsie Devlin was. But the old drunken cowboy with the portrait, having been temporarily drawn to the train, was now staggering through the mud toward the Royal. He deserved a chance to hang his picture.

Hewitt jammed his thumb into the bartender's belly so hard that he doubled the man over. "Inside, Fatty, and let's talk this over in peace and good manners. I am *so* tired of being sassed by snotty cheap help!"

The bartender turned white, no doubt having heard about Bill Anderson's bad luck last night. He backed into the saloon. Hewitt took time to give the old cowboy with the portrait a wink.

"Behind your bar, Fatty! There, that's better. Now, I asked you a question. Where is Mrs. Devlin?"

"Her and Paul went for a ride in their buggy. First good day we've had for some time, and—"

"Which way did they go?"

"Please now, Mr. Hewitt, don't you get me in bad! I heard they went out to the Fishhook, but you know what'll happen to me if she finds out I told you. She'd have me run out of town, that's what!"

"That's pitiful indeed, Fatty, but the time comes to all of us to decide whether we want to be mice or men. I'm sure you'll be more at home among the mice. Good night, sir."

So the Devlins were out at Carl Hohn's place, no doubt talking about a flour mill! When Hewitt left the Royal, he had to push his way through the crowd that had collected on the sidewalk. His portrait of the old cowboy, with the verse below it, was tacked to the wall just outside the door.

Not quite gentlemanly of me, Hewitt decided, listening to the vindictive laughter that hailed each delighted reading of the verse. But everything's fair in love and war. So there's going to be an eighty-car train of empties tomorrow, is there . . . ?

Frowning thoughtfully, he went to the railroad station and sent a telegram to a railroad detective he knew. He and Johnny Quillen were by no means friends, but they knew how to work together in the interest of justice *as they saw it.* Sometimes justice was not merely blindfolded, but hogtied and gagged.

From the depot, he went straight to the hotel. As he mounted the steps, stamping the mud off his boots, he looked back. "Tom Black" had followed him across the street, walking slowly, with his thumbs hooked in his belt. For a moment, he raised his head to look straight at Hewitt.

Their eyes met. It was "Tom Black" who first dropped his gaze. The blacksmith was right, Hewitt decided. The fugitive did indeed look like a man in the advanced stages of tuberculosis, with nothing to look forward to in life, and nothing to regret in leaving it. Of such damaged materials were killers made.

Hewitt went inside and ran upstairs. The door to number 12 had been replaced, and so had the lock. His key did not fit, but the door was open and his new key lay on his dresser. He locked the door, undressed, got into bed, and made up his mind to awaken at exactly eight-thirty.

That would give him time for supper before he began, with a crystal-clear conscience, his duties as deputy town marshal of Dunsmuir, Kansas.

CHAPTER FIVE

Marshal Hall brought him his badge as he sat at table in the dining room. Ernie Hall looked like a man who was having worried second thoughts, but he had made up his mind and was not ready to change it. "If these cowboys make up their minds to start trouble," he said, as Hewitt pinned on the badge, "I reckon there's nothing you nor me nor anybody else can do."

"There's always one thing," Hewitt said.

"What's that?"

"Close the saloons."

"I doubt I got the power to do that."

"Ernie, if there is 'clear and present danger' of public disorder, as the judges say, there isn't much you can't do to prevent it. I'm sure the courts would back you."

The old marshal smiled. "Wouldn't Mrs. Devlin have a fit, though!" The smile died. "Wouldn't it only make things worse, to cut off their liquor?"

"It's a chance you may have to take."

"Do what you think has to be done. Damn that railroad! If it would only move the herds out of here, this town would quiet down again. When you're through eating, Mr. Hewitt, I'll make the rounds with you once."

"I'm 'Jeff' to my friends."

"All right, Jeff. Damned if I don't feel better already, having you on the job when I'm asleep!"

They left the hotel together. The weather had changed again. It still was not raining, but a raw, clammy breeze had almost emptied the sidewalks. Their boot heels echoed loudly on the plank sidewalk, and then came silence as they crossed a short side street in the mud.

They were halfway across when Hewitt saw, in the darkness of the empty side street, a darker something that moved. It was instinct and habit, not reason, that made him clutch Hall's shoulder and snarl at him, "Down, get down! We're being ambushed."

They dropped, but Hall did not drop soon enough. The whole side street seemed to light up as two guns went off, almost at the same split-second. Hewitt heard the unforgettable scream of a bullet past his ear.

The other one thumped into Hall, with a sound just as unforgettable. Hewitt felt the marshal go limp. He heard him moan and snap his teeth and stiffen again, without ever losing consciousness.

Hewitt, squatting on his heels in the mud, already had the .45 out of its trick holster under his coat. He squeezed off three shots as fast as he could pull the trigger. He heard a man scream, a high, wavering sound that keened out and stopped abruptly.

"*Ah-h-h-h!*"

Just that, and then silence. No answering shot came. The owner of the second gun had already gone speeding up the muddy side street toward the vacant lots behind the buildings.

The marshal was grunting in his effort not to moan. The

sidewalks were suddenly full, and one man had a lantern. Hewitt roared orders at him.

"Bring that lantern here, and somebody go bring a doctor. Ernie Hall has been ambushed, and I think he's hurt badly."

They crowded around him. By the lantern's light, Hewitt saw an evil-looking wound where the marshal's neck and shoulder met. It would be painful, painful as hell. It would be a slow healer. But it was not fatal.

"Who would bushwhack Ernie? He's fair to everybody," someone was saying.

"They wasn't shooting at him," came the answer. "They was shooting at that goddamn Pinkerton."

"I'm quite sure you're right, except that I'm not a Pinkerton," Hewitt replied.

"You're the one got him shot," the same surly voice said.

"Wait till we've got Ernie in a doctor's care, and then try my patience with your big mouth."

Marshal Hall struggled to his feet. "Listen, all of you! Mr. Hewitt's the law until I'm on my feet again. I'm all right now, Jeff. Bleeding a little, but I don't mind a little sting. Let's see if you hit anybody."

The man with the lantern walked through the mud of the side street with it. The light suddenly disclosed the body of a man on his face in the mud. Someone knelt to turn him over.

"Square in the chest! Mighty lucky shooting, I'd remark," someone said.

"When you know how to shoot, you can count on luck now and then," said Hewitt. "Anybody know who he is?"

"Just some riffraff cowpuncher."

"Any idea who he works for?" No answer. Hewitt chuckled and went on, "The Fishhook, isn't it? You're such a hell of a bunch of hotheads when it comes to jumping one Pinkerton, but you lose your guts when it's the Fishhook, don't you?"

The doctor came running, carrying his own lantern. Hewitt liked him immediately. Dr. James Hanrahan was young and slight and boyish in build, but he had a man's bass voice with the sting of command in it.

"Hold still, Ernie, you old idiot! You've got some torn muscles I have to stitch up, but you'll live to play the fool for an ungrateful town another day. A man your age, playing peace officer for these lawless ranchers! Somebody help me get him to my place."

"The hell with you! Get him there yourself," someone said.

"I can walk," Marshal Hall said. "I don't need help."

He pushed the doctor's hand away. Here is one tough old man, Hewitt thought admiringly . . . He had to catch Hall's arm to steady him, once he was on his feet. But then the marshal insisted on looking again at the dead man, before having his wound treated.

"Fishhook rider, all right," he said, when the lantern-light showed him the face of the dead man. "I seem to remember seeing two of them."

"Yes. The other one got away," said Hewitt.

"Talk to Carl Hohn about him, Mr. Hewitt. It's time the Fishhook stood to answer for what its men do."

"It'll be too late for that. Whoever it was, he has long since wiped out his own trail," Hewitt said. "Let's get you up to the doctor's house."

The doctor's wife opened the door for them. She was young, but already matronly looking, competent, and not afraid. She had scissors ready to cut off the marshal's shirt. By the time the doctor was ready to sew up the wound, she had the tray of instruments ready.

"So!" said the doctor, as he worked, with a curious glance at Hewitt. "You're the Pinkerton man."

"I am not a Pinkerton man," said Hewitt.

The doctor's glare challenged him. "You look like one, act like one. I've seen the Pinkertons in action, breaking strikes in the coal country, and spying out the men with guts to fight back. I hate their guts."

"Many people do."

"And you have no shame about it?"

"I told you, I'm not a Pinkerton man, Doctor."

"Well, a Pinkerton may be just what we need here," Dr. Hanrahan sighed. "This fool is going to get himself killed, playing policeman. It takes someone fox-wise and wolf-mean to do the job, like a Pinkerton."

"I'm mean. I don't know how wise."

"You can certainly shoot. I already have one patient who is your victim."

Hewitt said irritably, "He shot his way into my room. I fired at a shadow. No man can shoot well enough to shatter a humerus intentionally in the dark."

"So you know the names of the bones, do you?"

"I make it my business to know what I need to know."

"Oh? What else do you need to know, sir?"

"Well, for one thing—if you're betting your savings on a flour mill being built here, you're a curious sort of fool for an educated man."

By the quick reaction of Mrs. Hanrahan, Hewitt knew he had scored another hit in the dark tonight. The doctor, however, looked around coolly.

"What do you know about a flour mill?" he said.

"That it will never be built."

"What's this about a flour mill?" said Ernie Hall.

Hewitt gave the doctor a chance to reply. When he did not, Hewitt said, "It's a chance for everyone to get rich overnight. You were probably left out, because you'd ask too many embarrassing questions. It takes two things to be invited to join this get-rich-quick scheme. One is money. The other is the same country stupidity that bets a pat hand, in a game where the stranger with the beady eyes always draws four cards."

"Explain that, please," the doctor said. "I'm not a poker player."

Hewitt said patiently, "The hayseed with money gets into a 'friendly' game in the back room of a barn somewhere. He wins a few dollars, and then suddenly is dealt a pat, jack-high or queen-high straight."

"Is that a good hand?"

"Better than some! Only one man stays against him, the gimlet-eyed gent who keeps only one card. Not much chance he can fill a hand by drawing four, is there? Only when the hayseed has shoved in his stack, the other man's cards turn out to be all of one suit!"

"And that's a better hand?"

"It's called a flush, and it beats a straight. How much are you in for, in this flour mill?"

"I could raise four thousand dollars. That is the sum we

have discussed. Tell me—why do you think the flour mill will never be built?"

"How much is Carl Hohn in for?" Hewitt countered.

"I understand that he and the Devlins are putting up ten thousand each. The total cost of fifty thousand."

Subtract the ten thousand the Devlins are supposed to put up, Hewitt thought, and you come out with a cool forty thousand dollars again! Just what vanished from Mrs. Cushman's estate. Elsie's getting into a rut . . .

"Who is going to run the flour mill, Doctor? That's the key man in any proposition of this kind."

"Mr. J. Courtney Taylor of Laramie, Wyoming. He is in the mortgage business, but he comes from an old flour-milling family."

"Will you hold off on your investment, until I find out about Mr. J. Courtney Taylor?"

"I thought you weren't a Pinkerton!"

"I'm not. Neither am I idiot enough to invest in anything without looking up the key man. If you're dying to drop four thousand, go ahead. But I'm sure I can find out something in twenty-four hours."

"I am in no hurry to invest, and I'll appreciate any help you can give me. I'm sorry, Mr. Hewitt, but I was predisposed against you by having to cut off a man's arm today."

"As I was predisposed against him, when he shot his way into my hotel room. How is he, by the way?"

"He seems to have no will to get well. He has had a hard enough life with two arms. What will he do with one?"

"Has he had many visitors?"

"Not one."

"Not even Tom Black? Not even Amanda Rody?"

The doctor was plainly startled. "Why would Amanda Rody come see him?"

"He was looking for her when he shot his way into my room. He was ready to kill her for cheating on him."

"The hell he was!" Ernie Hall growled.

"You look surprised, too, Doctor," Hewitt said. "I judge you've always been friendly with Carl Hohn."

"By no means."

Hewitt shot a quick glance at Mrs. Hanrahan, and saw the snapping of her eyes, the angry pink that flushed her cheeks. "I see! Mrs. Hanrahan and Mrs. Hohn have been friends, is that it?"

"That's it."

"And you've been upset because Hohn, old fool that he is, has been playing the gallant with Amanda Rody."

"I thought you weren't a Pinkerton. But you're right, of course. Amanda Rody has turned that old fool's head, until he doesn't know the pump handle from a mule's tail. Now you tell me that my one-armed patient is her admirer too! You keep your eyes and ears open as you go through life, don't you?"

The doctor did not seem to expect an answer. He finished bandaging Hall's wound, and handed him an envelope containing a few tablets.

"Take one every three hours, if the pain gets too bad. I'll have a look at it again tomorrow, Ernie. Now let me hitch up my horse, and I'll take you home."

"I can walk. Mr. Hewitt can help me," the marshal replied.

"I'm sure he can. He is a very helpful man," the physician said thoughtfully.

Hall did not speak until they had almost reached his little house, almost at the other end of town.

"A lot going on around here that I don't know about, Mr. Hewitt," he said suddenly.

"You hadn't heard about the flour mill?"

"Not one word! I know that Carl Hohn has raised a lot of cash lately. He's a quarrelsome old fool, but there has never been any real harm in him before. I'd hate to see him picked clean, at his age. Look here—is Mrs. Devlin promoting a fake flour mill? Is that it?"

"That's my guess."

"Who gets the rest of Carl's money? Because he has raised a lot more than ten thousand dollars!"

"My guess is that Elsie underestimated how much the old fool was good for, when she set up this deadfall. She brought Mandy Rody in to help bait the trap, and the girl may be double-crossing her."

"By getting some of Carl's money herself?"

"It would be characteristic. Regardless of what you have heard, there is very little honor among thieves."

"All this going on under my nose, and I haven't a smell! You, a perfect stranger, come to town and turn it inside out. I just wonder, Mr. Hewitt, why you *really* stopped here. But I won't ask, sir—I won't ask! Good night, and thanks for all you have done."

From Hall's house, Hewitt went straight to the railroad depot. It was closed, but he gave a small boy he met a dollar to take a note to the station agent, at his house. It said:

I wish to send a telegram, and will pay you $10 to get it off within the next hour. I'll be on the street somewhere, if you'll be so kind as to oblige me in this matter.

The street seemed curiously deserted, as he began his first patrol as a deputy marshal. At the Royal, the caricature of the cowboy, with its derisive verse, had vanished from the outer wall. He looked inside. It was eleven o'clock, and the saloon should have been jam-packed. It was less than half full, he estimated. There was no sign of Paul or Elsie Devlin. The same fat bartender was on duty behind the bar.

Hewitt went inside. He understood the reason for the lack of trade when he saw the hand-lettered sign on the bar: No BEER UNTIL TRAIN COMES IN TOMORROW.

He dropped a ten-dollar gold piece on the bar. The bartender held up two bottles with a questioning look. Hewitt nodded to the bonded brand. The bartender set out the bottle and a glass.

"Where are Mom and Paulie tonight?" Hewitt said.

"Don't start it with me, now!" the bartender said. "That was a dirty, filthy trick to play on a lady."

"On a lady, yes indeedy. Is Carl Hohn about?"

"You don't see him here, do you?"

"How about Mandy Rody?"

"Why, she never comes in here!"

The station agent came panting through the door. Apparently he too had heard how "that Pinkerton man" scattered the gold pieces about. Hewitt drafted a wire to Conrad Meuse, his faithful if stodgy partner back in Cheyenne:

SEND IMMEDIATELY ALL INFO J. COURTNEY TAYLOR
LARAMIE MORTGAGE BROKER ESPECIALLY BACKGROUND
IN FLOUR MILLING RUSH SOONEST MOST URGENT.

"It'll be in Cheyenne in three hours. How early it'll be
delivered there, I can't say," the agent said.

"The addressee will receive it promptly," said Hewitt.
"If I can have his reply as promptly, I'll know how to
show my gratitude. And this is of course confidential."

"You bet! Minute your answer gets in, I'll get it to you
somehow."

The railroad man hurried out to send the wire. Hewitt
turned his attention back to his drink.

"Pretty quiet tonight, isn't it?" he said.

"Well, we're out of beer, and it kind of damped this
down when Ernie Hall got shot and that cowboy got
killed." The bartender seemed anxious to make friends.
He leaned closer. "You know, what I hear is that the
shot that got Ernie was really meant for you."

"You can hear anything. Do you know the name of the
assassin that I shot?"

"They called him 'Brownie.' I don't reckon that anybody knowed his real name. Hard drinker, I know that, and
he had the reputation of being a gunman. No more?"

Hewitt shook his head and pushed the bottle back after
one drink. The bartender put his change down. Hewitt
pushed a quarter back to him. The bartender shook his
head.

"Sorry! Mrs. Devlin says that nobody is to take tips
from you. She's really sore about that picture."

Hewitt felt distaste for what he had to do. The fat bartender was harmless in his way, but he was also probably

a good source of information. There was only one way to deal with him.

Hewitt's hand shot across the bar and closed on the bartender's shirt collar. He twisted hard, and said through his teeth, "Pick it up, Fatty, and put it in your pocket. You don't have to thank me, but by God, you will not refuse my good United States coinage!"

The bartender reached for the quarter. Hewitt let go of his collar.

"You trying to get me into trouble, Mr. Hewitt?"

"With Mom?"

The bartender winced. "Please, sir! She's just boiling about that picture."

"And you know why," Hewitt said. "It hits her right where she lives." He dropped his voice to a confidential level. "Oh yes, it's easy to admire Elsie until you get to know her, but surely you know her by now! Forget all you ever heard or knew about gentle, tender women. None of it fits her, now, does it? Or do you *like* being a flunky for a female tiger?"

Again the fat bartender winced. "Well, I sure don't like some of the things going on around here. Poor Mandy Rody, for instance. That is just terrible!"

You too, Hewitt thought . . . "Suppose I had some good news for Mandy," he said. "Where would I find her?"

"I'd be glad to pass it on, Mr. Hewitt."

"It's not that kind of news. I'll see her myself."

"Her room is always locked. You couldn't get in unless she unlocks it, and many a man has found out that she won't."

"I'm sure that's true, but where is her room?"

"Why, right next to yours! Number 10, in the hotel."

"Would she be there now?"

"She damn' well better be!" The bartender's eyes dropped in embarrassment. "Mrs. Devlin gave her hell today about something. I think it was about that young fellow you shot. I—I hate to see that girl in trouble, Mr. Hewitt. She's really a nice, sweet, quiet ladylike girl."

"I wonder if Mrs. Hohn would endorse that."

"Now, all that talk about Mandy and Carl Hohn is just dirty gossip! Mandy ain't that kind of a girl."

Hewitt put two silver dollars on the bar. "Time to size yourself up, Fatty. Just because you wear pants and walk on two legs doesn't mean you're a man. There are several kinds of two-dollar whores, you know, and you're in a foul and grubby business. I'll check in a little later, perhaps, after you've thought it over."

He flicked the two coins across the bar. The bartender let them jingle to the floor, and covered his face with his hands. Hewitt went out on the street.

One by one, he visited the other saloons. They were all out of beer. The frustrated cowboys were catching a night's sleep, for a change. At least, Hewitt thought with a smile, it's not raining tonight . . .

At the last little bar, the one nearest the livery stable, there was not a single customer. One man dozed behind the bar. On the wall behind him was the picture Hewitt had drawn earlier in the day, with the ribald verse below it.

Hewitt ordered a drink. "Risky, isn't it?" he said, nodding toward the picture.

The man shrugged. "Some of the boys grabbed it, when

Mrs. Devlin started screaming. They brought it here. I happen to think it's a fine work of art."

"Where's the fellow who sat for the portrait?"

"Mrs. Devlin's bouncers caught him and beat the hell out of him."

"Where is he now?"

The bartender looked at Hewitt's badge. "Afraid I forgot, if I ever knew."

"My friend, I'm the man who drew that picture."

"The hell you are! Well, don't worry about that poor fool. He'll be cared for until he's on his feet again."

"Who will take care of you, if you run into a slight case of bad luck?"

"We all live until we die, I reckon. Odd how things work out! Nobody ever had a bad word to say against the Devlins until today. Our leading citizens, you just bet they was! Now here comes a Pinkerton to town, and suddenly they haven't got a friend left in the world. Don't that strike you as mighty curious?"

"I am not a Pinkerton," Hewitt said, as he went out. "Good night and good luck. You may need it."

"I wasn't hatched yesterday. Good luck to youself! Even," the bartender called, "if you are a damned snooping Pinkerton."

Another friend made. An operative who could not make friends—many of them, and fast—was never going to be very successful in the business. I should have been a missionary, Hewitt thought, as he patrolled the street. The way I go about spreading sweetness and light . . .

CHAPTER SIX

By three in the morning, the town was empty, and the last saloon had closed its door. The old bellboy, Bob Kramer, was lurking in the shadows just outside the hotel. He made no sign to Hewitt, but he seemed pleased when Hewitt spoke to him.

"Evening, Mr. Kramer. Who has charge of the house keys here?"

"They're at the desk. You see Tom Black tonight?"

"No, why?"

"He's been prowling about somewhere. I seen him three times."

"He made sure that I did not see him. What room do Paul and Elsie Devlin have?"

"They don't live in the hotel. They got a nice little white house with a picket fence, up close to where the doctor lives."

Hewitt remembered having seen a white house with a picket fence. Not that it mattered, so long as the Devlins were not in the hotel.

"Do you have any errands you could run for the next hour or so? You might not want to be a witness, Mr. Kramer."

He left old Bob to puzzle it out. The clerk gave a start

and came awake as he stopped at the desk. Hewitt nodded good night and took a few steps toward the stairs.

The clerk put his head in his hands and went back to sleep. Hewitt tiptoed back to the desk, went behind it, and groped for the big ring of house keys. The clerk did not move.

He found the key to number 10 on his way upstairs. The second-floor hall was pitch-dark. He passed his own room, stopped at the next door. He verified the 10 on it by running his fingertips over it in the dark.

He fitted the key into the lock, turned it. The door still would not open. On the door to his own room, there had been no safety bolt, but there was one here. He did not think it would amount to much. It was not like Elsie Devlin to buy the best for her help.

He located the bolt by springing the door to find a firm place. He braced his shoulder blades against it, planted both feet, and pushed back.

The bolt yielded with a sharp but light ripping noise, as the screws came out of the soft wood. There was no sound inside the room. Hewitt stepped inside, closed the door, and locked it with the house key. In a moment, he could make out the shape of the sleeping girl by the faint light that came through the window blinds.

He located the bedside lamp, and silently removed the chimney. He swiped a match across his pants, touched the flame to the wick, and replaced the lamp chimney. The girl slept heavily, without stirring.

She lay on her side, facing him, a small girl with a tumble of black hair. Not the prettiest Hewitt had ever seen, but young and fresh-looking and wholly desirable. It was not hard to understand how a greenhorn kid like Slim Gurkey, *alias* Bill Anderson, would lose his wits over her.

Hewitt sat down on the side of the bed and took the girl's bare shoulder in his hand. He shook her and said softly, "Mandy. Mandy, wake up!"

She opened her eyes. He slid his hand up to her throat and whispered, "Be quiet, Mandy, and you won't be harmed. I'm going to talk and you're going to listen. Are you going to behave?"

"The Pinkerton man!" she gasped.

"Let's not waste time arguing about that. How serious are you about this Gurkey kid? The truth, Mandy!"

"About who?"

"He calls himself Anderson here, but I think you know who he is. He came clean with you, didn't he?"

"About what?"

Her sudden alertness told him he had scored. "About why he ran and changed his name. About the murder of Ed Batchelder, my dear."

"He didn't do that! He got roped into it!"

"By Charley Kenyon?"

He could see her decide that she had already said too much. He could not afford to waste time with her. His hand tightened a little on her throat, and his thumb found the pit under her ear.

Her pretty face constricted in a spasm of pain. Her eyes flashed a quick signal of surrender. He eased his grip. "Sorry, Mandy. I'll repeat the question. He was roped into it by Charley Kenyon?"

"Well, he was!"

"Who did the actual shooting?"

"Kenyon. Bill didn't even have a gun! He pawned it for ten dollars to get into a poker game."

They studied each other. She was still afraid, but this girl had been in tight spots before. She knew how to keep her head long after the average woman would have started shrieking.

"Why doesn't he cut loose from Kenyon, and tell what he knows? He could get off free."

"Charley would kill him. He would, believe me!"

"Gurkey is afraid of him?"

"You damn' right! So am I."

"Mandy, are you in love with Gurkey?"

The big dark eyes narrowed calculatingly. "I could like you a lot better. Don't be mean to me! Take care of me. I wouldn't be afraid of anybody, if you would."

He suddenly remembered the day when another woman, a striking, buxom blonde, had made almost the same plea. In a way, it had been even more persuasive, because Elsie Devlin was not the pleading type. He even seemed to remember a conviction that she really was in terror of her life—that she truly needed protection, probably for the first time in her life.

She was newly a bride then, but what good was Paulie Devlin, that handsome but weak and empty slob, to a woman in terror? It had taken all his iron self-control to shake his head smilingly, and reject her without letting her suspect how painful it was.

He shook his head smilingly at Mandy Rody. "Come on, girl—one thing at a time! Are you in love with him?"

"What difference does it make? Do you think I'm crazy, Pinkerton man? He only has one arm. He never had much chance in life with two."

"Sh-h! I'll do the talking. First, tell me what you know about the murder of Ed Batchelder, and then let's see how we can help you. Get to talking, honey! We haven't got forever, and I'm going to get the truth out of you, whether it hurts Gurkey or helps him."

She whimpered, "They were going to stick that fellow up, only he didn't have any money on him. That's all I know."

"Come now, Mandy! The killing—how did it happen?"

"Black or Kenyon or whatever his name is—he just went crazy and began blasting away, that's all! And you can ask around there and find out, Bill lost his gun in a poker game. How could he shoot anybody?"

"I see."

He frowned, thinking it over, unwilling to take her unsupported word, yet at the same time feeling fairly sure that he was hearing the straight story of the death of Jim Batchelder.

"Is that what you're here for? To catch Bill and Tom Black, I mean? That isn't what Mrs. Devlin thinks. She thinks that—"

"I know what Elsie thinks. Forget her! How much money has poor old Carl Hohn given you?"

"Oh—maybe a little over two hundred dollars."

He smiled scornfully. "Do you think I was born yesterday? I know how much he drew from the bank!"

"Oh, that," she said. "He bought a house in Topeka with

part of that money. He wants me to go live there, and he'll take care of me. Elsie says he's got to do more for me than that."

"Do you *like* him, Mandy?"

"That poor simple-minded old jackass? But how can I beat that deal? How much chance do you think a girl has got? I'm damned if I want to end up in a crib!"

Poor waif, Hewitt thought—old Hohn would be no bargain at any price. Neither is Slim Gurkey, but if he is what you want—

"Mandy, if Gurkey could be sure he would be let off without standing trial—if we could make a deal with the prosecutor for him to go scot-free for testifying against Kenyon—would he do it?"

"What good would it do him, with one arm? How's he going to make a living, if everybody knows he's a rat that snitched on his sidekick?"

"There are jobs a one-armed man can do, and you're a strong, healthy girl. Suppose you had a thousand dollars, and could get out of town without anyone knowing it—go to Kansas City and start a boardinghouse—"

She threw off his hand and cut in savagely, "Make it five thousand, you cheap skate. Look at what you're getting. I know the fees you gumshoe detectives get!"

"I might go a little higher, but you're in no position to dicker, Mandy my dear."

"Neither are you! Nobody on earth can talk him into turning Kenyon in—nobody but me! Listen, Pinkerton man—I know how to run a steam laundry. I worked in one from the time I was ten years old, until I was old enough to get a man to take me out. Five thousand will buy a steam laundry I know about in Kansas City, and five thousand is what it costs you to settle your murder case."

"Mandy darlin', I can buy you a steam laundry for from two thousand to twenty-five hundred, but I'll go as high as three thousand, and he has to make a complete statement before a notary public. It has to be good enough for me to make a deal with the prosecutor to get him off."

Their eyes collided. The girl's fell. "Not even thirty-five hundred?"

"Let's see how helpful you are, and how truthful Gurkey is."

"How are you going to work it?"

"I'll go see the doctor now. You get dressed. If it's all right to take you to the doctor's place, I'll do it before day-light. I think he'll hide you there until I can make arrange-ments to get you out of town. That may take a day or two. Now, who is a notary public that we can trust to attest Slim's statement and then keep his mouth shut? I can make it worth his while."

"Listen, I'll tell you how to find him. He owns a saloon, the one closest to the livery barn, and he's no friend of Mrs. Devlin's."

The man who had hung the portrait dedicated to "Mother Devlin." Yes, that one could be trusted. The girl flung herself out of bed, and in one flurry of motion pulled her nightgown off over her head. Naked as the day she was born, she ran lightly across the room to the dresser for fresh clothing. She turned and looked at him, quite calculatingly, before opening a dresser drawer.

"Pinkerton man, I know a better way to work this

whole thing out. I could forget Bill real quick, if you'd only take care of me," she said.

"Thank you, Mandy, but I'm afraid you're talking to a man without weaknesses," he said. And he knew he lied in his teeth as he said it.

She snatched something out of the drawer and gave him one long, dark look of terror and appeal. "Then get me out of here quick, before Mrs. Devlin finds out. She'll have me beat to death."

"You shouldn't have double-crossed her."

"About what?"

"How much did you *really* get out of Carl Hohn?"

Her eyes danced wickedly. "About four thousand. But you and I still have a deal for thirty-five hundred!"

"I live up to my deals, Mandy. See you."

By daylight, he had the document in his hands. Hewitt himself took the statement at the bedside, with Mandy, the saloonkeeper-notary public, and Dr. and Mrs. Hanrahan listening. The doctor and his wife then signed affidavits declaring that there had been no force, threats, or other duress applied. The statement said:

COMES NOW EZRA GODFREY GURKEY, also known as Slim Gurkey, also known as Bill Anderson, who being duly sworn, deposes and says:

Charley Kenyon, who now goes under the name of Tom Black, and I were working for the Rafter B, in Broken Bow, Nebraska, owned by James W. Batchelder. We were going to work there until we each had $50 saved up, and then go to Indian Territory. I am not sure of the date, but it was the first Monday in

August that Charley and I got into a poker game and gave some I.O.U.s, and I pawned my gun for ten dollars. We had to draw money to pay off our I.O.U.s, and Jim Batchelder can prove that he paid us.

So we had only about $15 left when we quit our jobs. Charley said he had an idea to get some money but he did not tell me what it was. After we quit, he said that Jim Batchelder's brother, Ed, owed Jim some money and was supposed to pay him $300. We would hold Ed up and take the money. I did not want to do it, but Charley said it would be easy, that Jim said his own brother did not have any guts.

We waited around and catched Ed when he stopped at the creek on Jim's place to water his horse. He didn't have much money on him, only about $3.50, and that made Charley Kenyon mad. Charley had this gun without any trigger, and was always practicing the fast draw. Charley said he knowed Ed had money because he was supposed to pay his brother $300.

Ed said he was just going over to tell Jim he couldn't pay him a cent. He began cursing, and said that between his wife and his brother, he never knew a moment's peace. Charley lost his head and fanned two shots into Ed in the chest. Ed fell back against his horse, and Charley moved a step closer and fanned two more shots into his chest.

Both of the last two bullets went into the horse and hurt it mortally. Charley made me lead it down to the creek before it could die, and he shot the horse while it was standing in the middle of the creek. We piled rocks on it so it would never be found. You can prove this by looking for the horse bones in the creek, also by where Charley buried the gun without any trigger.

He was afraid to have it on him, so he buried it under a cottonwood tree that is the corner post on the south fence of the Rafter B, near the township road.

I did not want to hold up Ed, and I did not have any idea that Charley would murder him. Then Charley said he would kill me too, if I left him. He would do it too. This is the truth so help me God. In witness whereof, I have hereunto set my hand and seal in the presence of two witnesses and a Notary Public.

                                            Ezra G. Gurkey

Hewitt got into bed just before daylight, with the document that would close the Batchelder case under his pillow. Mandy Rody would be safe with Dr. and Mrs. Hanrahan. A day or two of rest now, and then he could decide what to do about the Devlin case.

He heard a train pull in, heard the clatter as it set out a short string of empties. He had drifted off to sleep when there came a soft knock at the door of his room.

"Man to see you, Mr. Hewitt," came Bob Kramer's voice. "Won't give me his name, but he says you want to see him."

"Open up, Agate Eyes!" said another voice.

Hewitt got up and opened the door, with a reassuring nod for the old bellhop. A tall, heavy, slow-moving man who wore a low-crowned Stetson and a rumpled business suit came in. Hewitt closed the door.

They did not shake hands. "Happened to be up the line, and I was able to catch an extra bringing a few stock cars," Johnny Quillen said. "Come tell me what's bothering you, while you buy my breakfast."

Hewitt yawned. "I'm dead for sleep, Johnny."

"And I'm starved, Agate Eyes. I can still catch the train out of town."

"The railroad ought to be glad to buy your breakfast, since we're going to do them a big favor, Johnny."

"We are?"

"Yes. Why can't this town have more cattle cars?"

"Everybody's shipping. We try to take care of the big shippers, like Carl Hohn. We're trying to make up an extra train, just for Dunsmuir."

"No." Hewitt shook his head. "No more cars. Not one! Hold up every empty, Johnny."

The railroad detective scowled. "What are you up to, Agate Eyes?"

"Money! It's worth fifty dollars a day to you, every day that passes with no cattle cars for Dunsmuir."

"Can't be done. Hohn ain't just a cattleman. He's—"

"Yes, he and Mrs. Devlin are going to build a flour mill here, and be big shippers indeedy."

"That's supposed to be a secret, damn it!"

"I know. Now I'll tell you another one. There isn't going to be any flour mill."

"The hell you say!"

"Do your railroad a favor, Johnny. Look Elsie Devlin up. For openers, check with the Omaha authorities. They're still wondering where forty thousand dollars went. She's the world's number-one woman swindler, and she's mining this old fool of a Hohn with a pick and shovel. Your division superintendent is going to look like a bigger jackass than Hohn, if he takes this flour mill seriously. Do you want that to happen?"

Quillen said thoughtfully, "They're talking about a fifty

thousand dollar investment in this flour mill, and you offer me fifty dollars a day. Shame on you!"

"I'm on an expense account, Johnny. I'm helpless."

Johnny Quillen pointed his thick finger at Hewitt. "I don't know what you're up to, but suppose you close your deal in a couple of days. I make a hundred bucks, and these cowboys lynch me because I can't produce cars."

"I was going to offer you a slight retainer, in addition to the fifty a day," Hewitt said, with dignity. "I've got two passengers who must board one of your trains to Kansas City in secrecy, somewhere outside of town. I'd go as high as two hundred dollars."

"Five hundred."

"I just can't!"

"Agate Eyes, how do I persuade them to hold up the cars? I'm risking a good job. I never knew you to lie about something like this flour-mill deal, but there's always a first time. Five hundred, dear boy."

Hewitt threw up his hands. "All right, but I haven't got it on me. Meet me at my outfit at the livery barn at eleven o'clock. Let me get a little sleep, while you hold up those cattle cars!"

"What'll I tell them, to justify it?"

"Tell them you're working on a big swindle here, about the flour mill. Scare the hell out of them! I'll give you all you need to back up your bluff. I'll go as high as a thousand-dollar guarantee to you, no matter what happens."

"That's more like it. That's a deal, Agate Eyes."

Quillen went out. Hewitt locked the door behind him, and got back into bed with Slim Gurkey's affidavit rustling comfortingly under his pillow. He shook his head sadly at the deterioration he thought he had beheld in his old friend, Johnny Quillen. Johnny's slipping, he thought. I was ready to go as high as two thousand, if I had to . . .

CHAPTER SEVEN

Hewitt slept late, and awakened with a tired feeling that he had experienced several times lately, and which he regarded as a danger sign. He had never regarded his work as the most important in the world; yet while he was on a case, he had always been able to stay completely wrapped up in it. There was no time for fatigue or boredom. That always came later—after the job was done.

He whistled for Bob Kramer, and ordered steak, three eggs and a huge pot of coffee sent up to his room. While he shaved, he tried to shake off the sense of weariness. He had to make a real effort, to drive out of his mind the thought of how nice it would be to dump the whole mess and retire. Why go on with the hard work and the risk? He had enough money to retire. What was the point of—?

There was a knock at the door. "Come in, come in, Mr. Kramer! You're letting my breakfast get cold," he called irritably.

The door opened, but it was the railroad station agent, not the old bellhop. "Got a telegram from Cheyenne for you, Mr. Hewitt. I brought it over myself, the minute I got through taking it down."

Hewitt put the razor down to tip him and thank him. Bob Kramer arrived with the breakfast tray. Hewitt hurriedly finished shaving, and read the telegram as he wolfed his breakfast. The sense of fatigue and boredom vanished. Back came the excitement of the chase. He felt like a good hunting dog that had come upon fresh scent.

His partner, Conrad Meuse, was unimaginative but thorough. He had forwarded to Hewitt everything he needed to know about Mr. J. Courtney Taylor, distinguished mortgage broker and flour-mill expert:

SUBJECT ARRESTED GRAND THEFT LARAMIE BUT BROKE JAIL AND IS FUGITIVE STOP RECORDS SHOW NO MILLING BACKGROUND STOP LARAMIE SHERIFF SAYS SUBJECT SERVED SEVEN YEARS EMBEZZLEMENT KENTUCKY STOP UNABLE VERIFY BUT BELIEVE TRUE STOP IF HE SHOWS UP THERE BELIEVE LARAMIE POSTING FIVE THOUSAND REWARD STOP SUBJECT BELIEVED ARMED AND WILL SHOOT TO KILL TO AVOID ARREST

Hewitt whistled. Rewards usually came to ten percent of the theft. Ten times five meant that Mr. J. Courtney Taylor had skinned somebody in Laramie out of fifty thousand dollars. He's not going to show up here, then, Hewitt decided. If he knows Elsie well enough to go into a skin-game with her, he knows she'd turn him in for a lot less than five thousand dollars . . .

Did Elsie know that her prize exhibit, Mr. J. Courtney Taylor, flour-mill expert supreme, had become a fugitive? Probably. No doubt that was the reason for the buggy ride out to Carl Hohn's place with Paulie yesterday. They would have some ingenious story to feed the old rancher, to keep him on the hook. The loss of a partner would slow Elsie down very little.

Hewitt now had three cases, not just two. There was money to be made out of J. Courtney Taylor, if he got in the way. Add that to the fee in the Batchelder case, and the possible share of a recovery of funds in Elsie's case, and this could be a rich haul indeed.

A slight chill went through him, a sensation of danger. Could three such fat cases just *happen* to come together in this drab little shipping town, Dunsmuir? Or was somebody going to a lot of trouble to get him? Hewitt had made his share of enemies in his time.

No, everything was logical enough, when you took into consideration the kind of people he was dealing with. Charley Kenyon and Slim Gurkey were a cinch to find disreputable jobs somewhere. Elsie was the key to the whole squalid mess. Her egotistical vanity was equaled only by her lust for money. She would attract characters like Charley Kenyon and Slim Gurkey—and J. Courtney Taylor— the way a dead carcass drew buzzards.

Hewitt put the telegram in the breast pocket of his coat, along with Slim Gurkey's affidavit, and walked briskly toward the livery stable. Clouds chased one another across a vivid blue sky. This was the kind of weather that made cattle restless, especially if they were hungry. That was why there were no cowboys on the street this morning. They were all busy out at the holding grounds.

Carrington, the stableman, pocketed his daily fee with a grin. "I don't reckon it'll scare you much," he said, "but there's some talk going around town against you, Mr. Hewitt. Nobody likes Pinkertons, and cutting off that cowboy's arm has got folks riled up somewhat."

"I expect many would join a lynching party, only there's a shortage of people to lead one," Hewitt said.

"Some truth in that, surely!"

"It's always the case. I have friends in town. You don't know about them, and they don't know about you. Thank you for your warning, but I'm not alarmed."

"Just so you know that you ain't the most popular citizen of Dunsmuir."

Hewitt set out his tools and got ready to do business. When he was sure Carrington was in the barn and out of sight, he pushed his tool kit back under the back endgate of his house wagon, and then leaned over it to sort his tools.

People who knew wagons admired the heaviness and strength of the running gear on this one. The box sat on solid oak bolsters, six inches by eight, with half-inch steel plates at each end. While Hewitt jingled tools with his left hand, he used his right to unscrew one of the steel plates. Only one studscrew held it. The others were dummies.

The plate came off. A hole had been drilled lengthwise through the sturdy oak bolster. There was an eighteen-inch section of gas pipe inserted in the hole, with a cork driven into its end.

Hewitt withdrew the pipe and carefully pulled the cork. A series of bright gold coins, double eagles worth $20 each, began spilling into his palm, forced out by the spring-loading at the other end of the pipe. He counted out twenty-five of them—the $500 he had promised Johnny Quillen—and then replaced the cork in the gas pipe and the pipe in the bolster.

On the smooth wood of the bolster were some pencil scratchings. He made a couple more beside them, and winced. This was his set of books for keeping track of Jim Batchelder's expense money. He was down to $7,800, but he was close to his game. The affidavit in his pocket could wind up the case, in fact.

Where lay his duty now? He was authorized to spend as much as $30,000, if necessary. He had not spent a fourth of that. He sighed deeply as he screwed the dummy end-plate back on the bolster.

It went against his conscience, to solve a case with so much good expense money still unspent. He was a disgrace to the detective's profession, if he—

"Are you the fix-it man?" said a sharp voice.

He turned, palming the $500 in gold into his pocket, and smiling his courtliest smile. A small, bright-eyed woman with gray hair had come up behind him. She was carrying a one-man crosscut saw in her hand.

"Yes I am, ma'am," he said, "but if you want any saw work done, the blacksmith is the man for you."

"I know that as well as you do," she snapped. "I'm the blacksmith's wife. He's like every other man. He won't do his own job, so long as he can put it off to do somebody else's. This saw needs filing and setting, and I want you to put it in shape so he can get our winter's wood in before winter hits, for once in his life."

"In that case, I'll be delighted to do it. There will be no charge, ma'am," said Hewitt.

"I'll wait for it."

"It may take some time, ma'am. Setting a saw is—"

"I know what the job is. I'll still wait."

He nodded genially, clamped the saw down, got out his

files, and set to work. She watched him with critical eyes for a moment.

"I reckon you know what you're doing."

"I think so, ma'am."

"So I reckon it wasn't no accident when you run head-on into Carl Hohn. You knowed what you was doing."

"No, I regret that very much. Mr. Hohn lost his temper, but he's a gentleman and—"

"The hell he is! My sister is married to him. It's over a year since I've seen her to talk to. He won't let her come see me, and he made it mighty damn' clear that I ain't welcome out there to the Fishhook."

"I'm sorry to hear that, ma'am." Hewitt gave her a sympathetic look. "What was it, some family dispute?"

"You know what it was! He's at that age, the old fool. Chasing after first one skirt and then another. Now it's that Mandy Rody. He's made himself a laughingstock over the whole county."

"I never pay attention to gossip."

"You paid attention to this! That cowboy you shot was looking for that self-same woman. Don't you try to pretend with me, Mr. Pinkerton man!"

Hewitt put his tools down and looked her in the eye. "I'm not a Pinkerton man. Why are you telling me this?"

She suddenly twisted her hands together and pressed them into her stomach, to stifle her own sobs. "I hoped you was. I hoped you could do something about that old fool that is ruining his own life and my sister's both. I can't pay you much. All we got saved up is fifty dollars. Is that enough to hire you to do something?"

"What could I do, ma'am?" She could not answer. He studied her a moment, and made up his mind. "How far can I trust you to keep a secret, ma'am?"

"Fur as you have to," she said brokenly.

"Then forget about Carl and Mandy. That's all I can tell you. That problem is coming to a quick end. Now, what worries me is that Hohn may take it hard. No one can make him go back to your sister. Indeed, he may take his disappointment out on her."

"Or on you," she said, when she could control her voice. "I tell you, that man is out of his head!"

"Don't worry about me. Just forget that I said anything."

"Mister, if there's anything I can do for you—"

"Just one thing. Let me finish your saw, so I can get to some other work."

"Oh, give me back that saw! Let my old man file it himself. When a man gets a certain age, the only way to keep him out of trouble is to keep him busy. Here, this is your pay."

She pressed a wad of crumpled bills into his hand. Hewitt counted them quickly. He took out a dollar and handed $49 back to her.

"That's more than my time is worth, ma'am. If I had anything to do with ending your worries about Mandy Rody, you don't owe me for it."

She took the money back reluctantly, picked up the saw, and left. Other clients came—no big rush, but enough to keep him busy and increase the weight of silver in his jacket pocket. All waited for him to do their little fix-it jobs. They had heard about "the Pinkerton man." They wanted to look him over themselves.

Johnny Quillen did not show up until noon. The big detective sat down on the wagon tongue and waited until the last client had gone, and they were alone.

"Mighty good disguise, Agate Eyes," he said then. "Count on you to find some way to make it pay."

"Honest work deserves a just reward," Hewitt said virtuously.

"Maybe. Myself, I been keeping the telegraph wires hummin'. I went out on a very spindly limb with the division super. He hated to give up on that flour mill. It meant *so-o-o-o* much to him!"

"But you persuaded him it was a fraud."

"Yes. Now I wonder if I done the right thing."

Hewitt took Conrad Meuse's telegram from his inner coat pocket and handed it to him silently. Quillen read it in silence and then handed it back.

"My goodness, but this flour-mill feller is a naughty one!" he said.

"Yes. Your division superintendent will wonder where you get all your information, won't he?"

"Yes, and I wonder where you get yours."

"Well, information is our stock in trade in our business, isn't it?" Hewitt sighed. "That isn't all I have for you, Johnny my boy. Here!"

He dropped the shining new gold pieces into the railroad detective's big hand. Quillen counted them rapidly and put them in his pocket.

"Now I think I sold out too cheap, Agate Eyes."

"Well, I imagine my credit is good with you now."

"Yes. There'll be a train in about seven-thirty tonight, with eighteen empties. There'll be no more until I say the word. It'll take about an hour to load out. Now, you said you had passengers you wanted to slip out of town. There's a place where the rails cross the wagon road about two and a half miles east of town. The train can stop with the caboose right on the road, if your passengers are there by about eight-thirty."

"Excellent! I'll make the arrangements."

"These passengers of yours—they wouldn't be Mandy Rody and this cowboy that got an arm amputated, would they?"

"My, my—you do pick up the gossip, don't you?"

"Yes. As I view the situation, you're holing Mr. Carl Hohn at the waterline, port and starboard. Cutting off his cattle cars and stealing his girl on the same day. I hear he works thirty men."

"Twenty-nine now, I believe."

"Oh yes, the one you shot. Twenty-nine is still enough to tear this town to pieces."

"Afraid so."

"How do you cash in, if the Fishhook outfit turns the town up on edge and puts a chunk under it?"

"I don't want to smoke Elsie Devlin out myself. I want her own neighbors to do it. Carl Hohn may be an old fool about Mandy Rody. But when he hears the truth about the flour mill, I have a hunch he's going to realize where all his troubles started."

"You seem to have a special kind of grudge against Mrs. Devlin, Agate Eyes."

Hewitt lighted another cigar and drew on it lightly. His eyes got a faraway look.

"Johnny, another old fool fell for the wrong woman once. That same woman tried to throw herself at me, and she was younger and a lot more beautiful than she is today. I kept my head. It wasn't easy. She was—she was—"

He fell silent. Quillen said, "I see. What happened to the other old fool that didn't keep his head?"

"They say he jumped off a building when she married Paulie Devlin. Now I'm wondering."

"Think somebody pushed him?"

"Could be."

"If you prove it, can you cash in?"

"I think so. There was a big fraud case."

Quillen stood up. "Better let me know plenty of time before the train gets in, if you want to ship your passengers. I have to arrange with the train crew."

Hewitt let the railroad detective go ahead of him. He took his time, putting away his tools, and then strolled slowly back to the hotel for his light noontime meal. Bob Kramer was lurking about the dining room. His eyes showed relief at seeing Hewitt, but he did not speak. Hewitt took his time eating, and then went upstairs.

He first unlocked and examined his own room. No sign of anything suspicious. He was unlocking Mandy's room next door, with Mandy's own key, when the old bellhop came soft-footing it up the steps.

"Mr. Hewitt, that's a good way to get yourself into a heap of trouble," he said sternly.

Hewitt opened the door and looked inside. The girl had not been able to pack much of her clothing in the one suitcase Hewitt would let her take to Dr. Hanrahan's house. Someone had been through everything else she owned. Her clothing was thrown in a heap on the floor. Dresser drawers had been turned upside down on the bed.

Hewitt closed the door, locked it, and offered the key to Kramer. "I found this. I thought it looked like a hotel key. I see I was right."

"Wouldn't do any good, I reckon, to ask where you found it?" Bob said.

"You reckon right. Someone seems to have been very badly upset by her departure from the hotel. Elsie?"

"Yes, and you can't blame her, Mr. Hewitt! She took that girl in, from practically right off the street. She give her a chance to get out of a life of shame—"

"By steering her to an old fool cattleman old enough to be her grandfather," Hewitt cut in. "Motherly old Elsie, always thinking of someone's welfare!"

Kramer flushed angrily. "All the same—"

"It's not all the same, Bob. The girl has had a hard life. Mrs. Devlin was using her, as she couldn't have used a girl who could afford not to get mixed up in a dirty business for money. You've been a poor man yourself. Take my word for it, it's far, far rougher on a woman! Mandy isn't ungrateful, because you don't owe gratitude for what Mrs. Devlin was doing for her. Just be glad she had a chance to escape, and the guts to take it."

The old man's face gradually cleared. "I reckon so. I just hope she got clean away, is all. Because Mrs. Devlin is just—just—well, I never seen her in such a rage! If she gets the idee that you helped Mandy get away—"

"Give her that key and tell her where you got it."

Kramer squinted at him. "What's the matter, you don't enjoy your life no more, or what?"

Hewitt laughed and clapped him on the back, and they were friends again. Hewitt returned to the livery stable and his outfit, where two clients were waiting for him with repair jobs. He caught a furtive, scowling signal from the stableman, however, and made an excuse to go into the office of the livery barn before beginning work.

"Doc Hanrahan stopped in this morning, to have me check the fit of his horse's collar," Carrington said.

"I imagine you'd be the right man for that," said Hewitt.

"Yes. He said to tell you, if I seen you, that his patients are coming along fine."

"Delighted to hear that."

"He said that Mrs. Devlin hadn't been to his house, but Mr. Devlin dropped around twice, to see if Mandy Rody had visited his one-armed patient."

"I see. Thank you, friend Carrington! Is there any way I could get a message back to the doctor, without exciting suspicion?"

"I go right past his place on my way home."

"Perfect! I want to rent a buggy with side curtains, and a dark team that can step right out. Another man will pick them up about dark. He won't give any name."

"How will I know it's the right man?"

"He'll have a tattoo on his right forearm, a coiled rattle-snake in green, and the words, 'Watch Out for Me If You Get Me Mad,' in red."

"I'll remember that."

"Tell Dr. Hanrahan that the same man will be at his

house with the buggy about seven o'clock. I need not add, friend Carrington, that only you and the doctor are to know about this."

Carrington did not want to take the gold piece that Hewitt urged on him. "Think of your kids!" Hewitt said.

"I am thinking of them, Mr. Hewitt. Hoping they never get caught in a dirty job like mine, where they have to be paid for doing what a man ought to do anyway."

"Do what you ought to do—yes, that's a good rule of life, and I'm all for it," Hewitt said. "But in my job, I long ago learned that if you can get paid for it, it's a good rule of life to accept. Money won't clean up a dirty conscience. But oh, it feels so good to a clean one!"

Carrington laughed as he took the money.

Soon after sundown, Hewitt descended the hotel stairs rapidly. He buttoned his coat and he hurried through the lobby of the hotel. Reaching the street, he walked swiftly to the hardware store in the next block.

He bought a lantern, and had it filled with kerosene. Carrying the unlighted lantern, he hurried on toward the livery barn. The sidewalks were too crowded for him to tell if he was being followed. No one (except himself and Johnny Quillen) knew how many empties would be on tonight's train.

But the cattlemen and their riders could all hope, at least until the train came in. After that—

At the stable, he took a fine saddle and bridle from his wagon, and saddled and bridled one of his own chestnuts. He led her outside and mounted, holding the unlighted lantern. He rode westward out of town at a smart trot, the mare up on the bit in lively fashion.

He had never ridden in this direction before. His horse wanted to run. Hewitt let her run for a quarter of a mile, and then pulled her down to a walk for another mile. Again he let her run for a while.

Where three cottonwood trees, now almost bare of leaves, grew beside the road, he reined the mare in and pulled into the deeper shadows under the trees. He sat his saddle until he heard, distantly, the train whistling into town. He checked his watch by the glow of his cigar, and smiled. Seven-forty, only ten minutes late.

He waited another hour and then lighted his lantern. He stood up in the stirrups and swung it slowly back and forth, in a wide arc, three times. Then, holding the lantern steady, he shouted as loudly as he could:

"Hi-you, hi-you-u-u-u!"

He waited a moment, then changed his lantern signal to a rapid up-and-down motion. He raised the globe of the lantern to blow out the flame when he heard the train whistle the highball signal before pulling out.

He waited until his eyes were used to the dark before turning back toward town. He saw them coming before they saw him—three men who plodded their horses slowly and uncertainly in the darkness.

"Howdy, men," he said genially. "Nice night for a little canter, isn't it?"

He heard one of them grunt an order. The three ranged their horses squarely across the road.

"Hold up there, Pinkerton man!" one called. "What you doing with that lantern?"

"I am not a Pinkerton man."

"I said—what you doing with that lantern?"

"Signaling."

"Who to?"

"Nobody," Hewitt said truthfully. "Now get out of my way, you clumsy idiots, before somebody gets hurt."

He swung his horse crosswise of the wagon road, to make sure they saw him snap the gun out from under his coat. Only one of the three tried to get at his gun—and he paused with his hand not yet clenched around the butt.

Hewitt said, "Who else wants to lose an arm? The light is bad, but it's better than it was in my hotel room the other night. I'll wing one of you and then kill the other two, if you try to make trouble for me."

There was one split-second when he thought one of them might try his luck. What had happened to "Bill Anderson," however, had given them a new outlook on things. They could face death, if paid enough for it, or fired up by anger. They could not face being crippled for life.

"One at a time, boys, hand over your guns. You first! Ah there, that's a good sense! Why get killed or maimed for the kind of pay you get?"

He emptied their guns and strewed them along the dark trail on the way back to town. It was no surprise that all three rode Fishhook horses.

There were no Fishhook men on the crowded sidewalks in town, however. Even walking swiftly, he still heard enough talk to know that Carl Hohn's outfit had got all the empty cars tonight. There was no grumbling, however.

These men were past the talking stage. It would not be safe for a Fishhook man on the street tonight.

A railroad detective could always get a room in a hotel, even if somebody else had to be evicted. Hewitt was not surprised to see Johnny Quillen going up the stairway of the hotel. He followed Quillen into his room, and waited while the railroad detective washed up before going to supper.

"My shipment get off all right?"

"Why, the lady complained that she was five hundred short, and when that lady complains, she don't leave you in doubt as to her feelings, Agate Eyes."

"And what did you tell her?"

"Why, I gave her your Cheyenne address, and told her to send her own address there as soon as she got one, and you'd send her the money."

"Good! I don't like to lose track of her, in case Gurkey has to testify against Kenyon in court. That was why I shorted her a little on the cash."

"I bet it was!"

"She's a fine girl!"

"She sure knows a lot of strong words!"

"She'll make Gurkey amount to something in life. Gives you a good feeling, doesn't it, to know you have helped make two young lovers happy."

Johnny Quillen merely grunted and began to roll up his sleeves at the washbasin. On his brawny forearm was the tattoo of a coiled rattlesnake, in green, surrounded by red lettering.

CHAPTER EIGHT

Hewitt stood in front of the mirror to pin on his deputy marshal's badge. He set his hat at an angle that tilted it slightly forward. He stuck a cigar in his teeth and cocked it upward. He put a flowered kerchief of pale silk in the breast pocket of his coat, and his shot-filled leather sap in his hip pocket.

To stop all cattle cars would explode this town under Elsie Devlin like a stick of dynamite. All very well, but an uncontrolled explosion was not what Hewitt wanted. It was time to assert his authority—to take control before the dynamite went off.

A fight was going on in the street when he went down to dinner. It did not seem to him that either cowboy was going to be seriously hurt, but it was as good a place as any to start. He took the lantern that hung just inside the front door of the hotel and went out into the street.

He handed the lantern to someone. "Hold this. Up high, now! Let's see what we're doing."

The street had dried only a little. The two cowboys were slugging away at each other flatfooted. Hewitt went up, took the cigar out of his mouth, and spoke sharply.

"Cut it out, boys! This has gone far enough."

They ignored him. He stepped behind one of the brawlers and used the tips of the fingers on his left hand to knock the man's hat off. His right swung the sap in a short, vicious circle at the man's bare head.

One fighter was down, felled like a steer in the slaughterhouse. The other kept lunging forward, unable to stop himself. He caught the sap lightly in the middle of his forehead.

"There'll be no more of this!" Hewitt announced sternly, to the crowd. "Things could get worse before they get better, and you fellows are fools if you take it out on each other. Slosh these boys, somebody, and then let's clear the street."

He walked down the street without looking back. One swift tour of the town showed him that all was quiet. He returned and went into the hotel dining room by the street door.

Paul and Elsie Devlin were at their table in the corner. Hewitt bowed to them as he hung up his hat. Devlin merely averted his big brown eyes. Elsie tried to stare him down, but did not return his bow.

He knew when they got up, when he was beginning his dinner. He ignored them until they stopped beside his table. He put his napkin down and stood up.

"Good evening, Elsie—Paulie. You're looking fit."

"Gave yourself away, didn't you?" said Elsie.

"In what way?"

"You once drew a picture of Seth Johnson—remember? Now I know you're that damned Pinkerton man! You drew the one of that cowboy and hung it on my front wall. That was a filthy thing to do, damn you!"

"I'm a working man, Elsie," he said. "I have my living

to make, and I'm a pretty good portraitist. Surely you can't begrudge me my little fees!"

Elsie's fit of blind temper was over. She had control of herself now. "What do you want?" she said.

"Money. Isn't that what everyone wants?"

"How much?"

"All I can get."

"Why are you at my throat, though? Do you want to ruin me?"

"Yes."

That made her catch her breath and almost lose her self-control. "Why?"

"Elsie, I could sympathize with a poor woman who is only trying to lay aside a little for her old age. But you're a hog! I keep remembering poor old Seth Johnson, a shapeless pile of broken bones and mangled flesh."

"How could I help what he did?" she said hotly. "That was so long ago! Don't you ever forget?"

"Not when a friend dies. Now I keep looking at poor old Carl Hohn—his wits gone, his money gone, and now his girl. What does he do now? Jump off a roof somewhere? Or will someone have to push him?"

Elsie and Paul looked at each other, and then Paul excused himself with a nod and left. Elsie pulled a chair up to Hewitt's table and sat down.

"I want to talk to you, Pinkerton man."

"I'm not a Pinkerton man," he said, sitting down.

"Whoever you are. Where's Mandy?"

"You'll never find her. She's my witness now."

"Witness to what?"

Hewitt merely shrugged. The woman leaned across the

table and smiled at him. From a few feet away, they might have been taken for sweethearts—at least close friends. Hewitt thought, And she might have fooled me with that smile, if I had not known her so well before . . .

"How much to get out of town?" she said softly. "Make me an offer!"

"We're not rich. We're making money. But our expenses are a fright. The Royal, this hotel—"

"Don't forget the flour mill," he cut in.

"Where the hell did you hear about the flour mill?" she was startled into saying.

"I've seen you operate before, Elsie. Next, you're going to tell me that everything is mortgaged. I don't doubt that a bit. Let the bank take part of the risk! But I'll make you a little bet, Elsie. I don't care how much property you own, or where it is, or how much debt is on it. I can tell you how much cash you could raise if you had to."

"Oh, you can!" she said. "All right, go ahead—tell me! How much cash could I raise?"

"About seventy-five thousand dollars."

"What? You're crazy! Why, we could barely—"

"Drop it, lady! I'll get thirty percent of all I can recover. Thirty percent of seventy-five thousand—round it off to about twenty-two thousand. I've got a partner who gets half. I never double-cross a partner," Hewitt said.

"Now do you see how impossible it is to make a deal with me? I'm after your hide this time, Elsie. I'm going to clean you out, and I'm going to enjoy every minute of it. And wherever Seth Johnson is, I hope he can see it and enjoy it too."

There was a brief glint of panic in her eyes, and then

anger. But as she stood up, she gave him her most brilliant smile and her hand. Hewitt stood up and bowed over the table to kiss the hand.

"Don't forget one thing. You're in my town now, Pinkerton man!" she said softly.

She swept out, giving him one last brilliant smile from the door. Hewitt thought it over as he finished his dinner. He had run down several killers, one defaulting bank president, a few gunrunners and some assorted horse thieves. Among the latter was a man who ran whole herds across the Mexican border. He lived on his own steam yacht, and maintained his own private Mexican army.

Yet Elsie Devlin was the first person ever to give Hewitt the uneasy feeling that he was betting against the stronger hand. She had the brains, and the tool-steel will it took to be a good criminal. But because she was a woman, she left Hewitt without his trump card.

Before letting a case go to a showdown, Hewitt had always made it a practice to let it be known that he was a dangerous man with a gun. He always whipped a man or two, to set an example. With a male adversary, these things implanted a doubt that often worked to Hewitt's advantage. Get a man afraid of you, and he was half whipped before the showdown came.

How did you impress a woman? It was something to think about. No, I'm not afraid, not at all, Hewitt decided. But she's bad, bad medicine . . .

Bob Kramer came to the table, carrying Hewitt's warm woolen mackinaw. "A frosty wind is blowing, Mr. Hewitt. You'll need this," he said.

Hewitt stood up and thanked him. Kramer held the

coat for him. Hewitt took a quick, sharp look about the room before putting his arms into the sleeves. A man was at a distinct disadvantage, putting on a coat.

Kramer muttered, "Ernie Hall wants to see you at his house, soon as you can make it."

Hewitt thanked him and went out. Immediately, he appreciated the coat. There was winter in the wind. He stepped into the Royal, where the sign was still up: NO BEER UNTIL TRAIN GETS IN TOMORROW. The few men in the place had the morose and cheerless looks of habitual drinkers, making their money last.

Elsie, on her high stool at the cashier's desk, was figuring on a piece of paper. She looked through him, rather than at him. Hewitt tipped his hat to her and went out, ignoring Paul, behind the bar.

At the saloon down the street, the drawing he had done of the old cowboy was gone, but the cowboy himself sat in a corner behind the stove, his head in his hands. Over the bar hung a sign, NO BEER. Hewitt raised his eyebrows at the bartender.

"Grocery stores are running out of things, too," the man said. "You're to blame, of course, according to the Devlins. No cattle cars in sight, either. Your fault."

"I see your portrait is missing."

"Yes. Fella took a fancy to it. Offered me fifty dollars. I might've got more, but I'm a cheap winner and never a big loser. Twenty-five dollars looked real big to me about then."

"The other twenty-five—?"

The barkeep nodded toward the man in the corner, who had not moved. "Look him over close, Mr. Hewitt.

This is how it goes with a man's bright ideas sometimes. Somebody else pays for them. That portrait ain't half as funny to me as it was yesterday."

Hewitt sat down and put his hand on the cowboy's shoulder. The man raised his head, and Hewitt got sick at his stomach. The cowboy had been cruelly, scientifically beaten within an inch of his life, by someone wearing metal knucks. His face was cut in a dozen places. His eyes were mere slits. His mouth was a pulpy mass.

"Do you look like this all over, cowboy? Did they give you the boots, too?" Hewitt said.

The cowboy nodded, unable to talk. He sat there with five five-dollar bills in his hands, in such pain that he was not quite conscious.

"Has he eaten anything?" Hewitt asked.

"We got some soup down him. He kept most of it down."

"Who does he work for?"

"The Circle G. They're camped four, five miles straight south."

"None of their boys in town?"

"No. I know what you're thinking—he'd be better off out there at his own cow camp. But he hasn't even got a horse. Hell, he hasn't even got a coat!"

Hewitt patted the cowboy's shoulder. "Friend, could you make it out to the Circle G camp, if you had a horse? Would they take care of you out there?"

The touch of a friendly hand seemed to give the beaten cowboy new life. "If I had a horse," he mumbled, "I'd be all right. The Circle G takes care of its men."

Hewitt helped the man to his feet, took off his own

mackinaw, and helped the man into it. "Tell George Carrington to mount you, and put it on my bill. Want me to ride out with you?"

"No. If I had a horse—but the Devlins own the livery stable, too, Mr. Hewitt."

"I know. You'll get your horse there, or I'll have somebody's hide, tail and all."

He watched the old cowboy walked down the street, unsteadily at first, but with a step that quickly became brisk. The saloonkeeper leaned in the door, chewing on a toothpick.

"Will George Carrington give him a horse?"

"I would bet on it."

The bartender studied Hewitt sharply. "I wonder if the Devlins realize what they're up against."

"I don't much care. Was it Paul bought the picture?"

"Yes. It was like crawling on his hands and knees, to have to do it. But he done it."

"Fine. Better close up now. You won't do any business anyway, and we don't want anybody to load up on the hard stuff. Lock your doors and go home."

"Is that an order?"

"Yes. Constitutional police powers."

"Anybody else closing down?"

"You're the first. It'll be a dry town soon."

The saloonkeeper merely nodded and spat out his toothpick, but Hewitt thought he was satisfied with the turn events had taken. Hewitt went back to the Royal, feeling the wind keenly without his mackinaw. There was no one on the sidewalk, but four riders were just tying in front of the Royal.

"Wasting your time, boys," Hewitt said. "The saloons are all closing for a while. We want to avoid trouble."

"Who does?" said one of the cowboys.

"I do. Now go on back out to your own camp."

The cowboy, a big, rangy, middle-aged man, stepped up on the sidewalk and tapped Hewitt on the chest. "Maybe you and the goddam Fishhook don't want trouble, but—"

"Hey Curly, that's the Pinkerton man!" one of his friends exclaimed.

"Right! Except that I'm not a Pinkerton," Hewitt said. "Let's go back to camp, now."

The man called Curly said stubbornly, "Paul Devlin is open. You mean the Fishhook people can drink, but the common people can't."

"I'm just going to close Devlin up. You boys come in and have one drink on me, before I do."

They followed him inside. Hewitt put a silver dollar on the bar. "Paulie, some of your best for my friends, and then lock up. I'm closing all the saloons until further notice."

Devlin looked quickly at his wife. Hewitt did not bother to turn to see how Elsie took it.

"Suppose you take your friends somewhere else to drink," Devlin said. "Keep this kind of riffraff out, and there's no need for anybody to close down."

Hewitt said softly, "Close up, Paulie. I won't tell you again."

Devlin stooped quickly, reaching for the gun or billy club that was behind every frontier bar. Hewitt jumped until his belly was across the bar. He chopped Devlin sharply on the back of the neck with his fist. He heard Elsie scream and saw Devlin sag to his knees.

Devlin came up with a foot and a half of smooth hickory pitchfork handle in his hand. The end of it, of course, would be drilled and loaded with several ounces of shot, well tamped in and sealed with melted lead.

"Been waiting for this, Paulie," Hewitt said happily. He went on over the bar and took the club on his shoulder as Devlin got to his feet. He could almost feel sorry for Devlin, if he felt as terrified as he looked. He found the softness of Devlin's belly with a left, and then another left.

Devlin doubled up, choking for breath. Hewitt brought his knee up and jammed Devlin's face down on it with both hands. He let Devlin straighten up and lean on the bar until he could breathe again. He heard Elsie behind him, and turned in time to see her leaning across the bar with a gun in her hand.

"Let's not!" he said. He swiped at her hand and sent the gun skittering down the bar to the floor. He turned to Devlin and began firing fists into him, where they would cause the most pain and make lasting marks without knocking him out. A step at a time, he drove Devlin out from behind the bar. He saw Elsie coming at him with a knife, and turned his back on Devlin to warn her.

"Don't try it, Elsie! I'll take it away from you and use it on Paulie. Drop it!"

When he reached for her wrist, she dropped the knife where Devlin could have picked it up. Hewitt contemptuously let it lay where it had fallen. Devlin was reeling blindly on his feet. Hewitt caught him by the belt and held him up while he went through his pockets one at a time.

He found it in the right-rear pocket, with Paul's hand-kerchief—a small chunk of bright steel with four finger-holds in it. You could kill a man with these knucks, with one blow in the temple. Or you could use it lightly, and leave a man's face a mass of scars for life.

Hewitt held up the knucks to Elsie. "All anybody has to do is see these, and they'll know who butchered the poor devil in the picture. People don't like that, Elsie!"

She began weeping brokenly. "Paul had nothing to do with that. Let Paul alone, Pinkerton man. My God, look at the way his nose and mouth are bleeding!"

Hewitt snapped his fingers at the other bartender, and then looked back at Elsie. "A drink for my friends, and then close up for the night." He tossed the steel knucks to one of the riders that had come in with him. "Here, a little token of Devlin hospitality. Keep it under your pillow, to remember them by."

They grinned at him, tossed down their drinks, and followed him outside. Without a word from Hewitt, they mounted and rode out of town. Hewitt stopped at two more saloons with the word, "Close up! Anybody looking for hard liquor at this hour only wants trouble, and that's what we want to avoid."

They were glad to close up. This was the worst fall shipping season any could remember. Only the Royal had made money this year.

Hewitt walked swiftly through the dark to Ernie Hall's house, feeling keenly the cold breeze. The marshal's wound was healing, but it was at the painful stage where he could neither stand up nor lie down. He was propped up on a chair with his head twisted to one side, in discomfort but no real pain.

"Mr. Hewitt, I've got nothing to do but think, and I don't like what has happened to our town," he said.

"It won't last," Hewitt said. "It will be a good place to live in again."

"Not if a bunch of rowdy cowhands get liquored up and tear it apart! I wish you and me could go out there and close up the saloons. More I think of it, the better I like that idee."

"Don't worry, Ernie. The saloons are closed."

Hall stared at him. "They are? Didn't nobody give you no trouble?"

"I had to pound on Devlin a little, before he saw the logic of it, but we came to a full agreement."

"Does Mrs. Devlin know about it?"

"She participated in the conference."

The old marshal squinted at him angrily. "No use trying to pump you, I reckon. Well, so much for closing the saloons. Let's go onto my next thought. I think we ought to set down and talk to Carl Hohn, and try to make him see that he ought to share the railroad cars."

"There won't be any to share for a few days."

"*What?*"

Hewitt chuckled. "The less you know about it, the better, but there won't be any empty cattle cars for a while. This won't hurt the other outfits, because they haven't been getting cars anyway. It will hit Hohn where he lives."

"What'll he do about it?"

"Scream to Elsie Devlin."

"What'll she do?"

"Nothing she can do. She has had influence with the railroad because of the flour mill. The railroad now knows that there isn't going to be any flour mill. Here, read this."

He gave the marshal his partner's telegram. "There's the 'milling expert' who was going to help them shake this town so hard its socks would fall off. I don't know if Elsie knows that this fellow has stubbed his toe, or not. But don't worry, the railroad is alerted."

"You do get around!" Hall said, handing the wire back. "Looks like I'm missing all the excitement and fun."

"It's better this way," Hewitt said, rising. "The man who lights the fuse is never popular. I can stand a little unpopularity. When it's over, and I'm gone, you can get all the credit for appointing me, and none of the blame for what I have to do."

"Well, it will keep me from feeling sorry about my wound, anyway," Hall said.

Hewitt returned to the deserted main street. As he passed the hotel dining room, a bulky figure came out and called his name. Hewitt stopped.

"Evening, Johnny."

"Cold night without a coat, Agate Eyes, ain't it?"

"Yes. A man has to keep moving to keep warm."

"Did you lend your coat, or was it stole from you?"

"It was a loan," Hewitt said, feeling a chill colder than any wind could produce.

"You won't want it back. Got some holes in it, and it's all blood-soaked."

"They got him," Hewitt sighed, feeling sick.

"Yes. Livery-stable man says he heard four shots, right

after this fella rode out. He got out in time to see two horses getting away. The fella was shot in the chest. He wasn't armed. They just gunned him down."

"How is Carrington taking it?"

"Why," said Quillen, "it seems that you sent word he was to supply this cowboy with a horse. He's got his share of nerve, but not enough for that. He put him up on one of your horses, and told him to send the horse back tomorrow.

"Your own chestnut horse, Agate Eyes, and this fella had on your mackinaw coat. I don't think they shot this fella for having his portrait done. I think they thought they were shooting at you. At least I'd call it a pretty strong hint."

CHAPTER NINE

The old cowboy, with four bullet holes in him, had been laid out in the livery stable. Any one of the shots would have been fatal. Someone had already ridden out to notify the Circle G camp.

By morning, the entire outfit was in town—but it consisted only of Haney Gordon and four men. Not a big outfit, by any reckoning. Gordon learned that Hewitt had already been over the ground with the first daylight.

"From the tracks," Hewitt reported, "I'd say he was holding the horse down to a walk, probably because he hurt all over. There were two ambushers. They sat their horses quite a while, back in the sumac along the road. When he got close enough, they just—cut him down. Then they left the road and crossed the railroad tracks. That's as far as they left visible sign."

"They knowed the country, or they couldn't of crossed the tracks. You dodge a lot of fences that way, but you have to know the road," Gordon said.

He was a work-bent man who looked sixty, although Hewitt took him to be in his early forties. Hewitt said, "I don't have the slightest suspicion they were strangers, Mr. Gordon. I'd say they were Fishhook men. I believe

I could name one of them. What was the dead man's name?"

"Never did hear it. We called him 'Jers,' because he came from New Jersey."

"What kind of man was he?"

"Hard worker. He liked jokes and he liked to argue, but there was no meanness in him. I wish you wouldn't be so free to blame the Fishhook. Carl Hohn is an old fool about women, but if he had any killing to do, he wouldn't *send* to have it done. He'd *lead* his firing squad."

"I don't think it was Hohn who sent them. They weren't after your man Jers. He was wearing my coat and riding my horse. And I promise you, Mr. Gordon, someone will pay for it. Where did you plan to bury him?"

"Why, I don't know. I'm short of money, and—"

"I'll foot the bills. Bury him here in the town graveyard, and order a stone for his grave. And I believe I would wait until afternoon, to let word get around. Let's see if anybody else comes to the funeral."

Long before noon, the town was full of grim and silent riders, not one of them from the Fishhook. Hewitt did not attend the burial services. He took just one look at the crowd that had come to town to bury a nameless rider, and hurried to the railroad depot to send another message to his partner, Conrad Meuse, in Cheyenne:

NEGOTIATE SOONEST WITH CUSHMAN HEIRS OMAHA FOR PERCENTAGE RECOVERY EMBEZZLED FORTY THOUSAND STOP DEMAND FORTY PERCENT BY WIRE AND SETTLE FOR THIRTY STOP BELIEVE CAN BLOW CASE WIDE OPEN IN WEEK OR TWO WITH COMPLETE RECOVERY BUT MAKE SURE HEIRS UNDERSTAND NOBODY ELSE CAN

Johnny Quillen showed up just as Hewitt was finishing the wire. "Big funeral?" Hewitt said.

"Close to two hundred," the railroad detective said.

"No whiskey and no railroad cars. Nothing for them to do but sit around stone-sober and think."

"About what?"

Hewitt handed him the telegram before thrusting it through the wicket to the agent.

"I see," Quillen said. "Big embezzlement, by the gods of old Ireland! Big enough for a three-way split."

"Depends on what you've got to offer."

"Let's go set in the sun and meditate, Agate Eyes. You're a cold-blooded plotter, but you lose your point of view when your feelings get tangled up in a case."

"Mine are tangled up in this one."

Quillen nodded and began walking toward the wood-fenced cattle pens beside the tracks. "Bad business, to get personally upset about a job. Let's climb up here for the sun and the view."

No use asking Johnny to come to the point. Quillen climbed to the top of the wooden fence, and Hewitt climbed up and sat beside him. Inside the eight-foot fence, steers milled restlessly. They were hungry and thirsty, and a long way from home.

"You don't calculate that Mother Devlin hired them boys to kill that old cowboy, do you?" Quillen asked.

"No. She'd steal the gold out of your teeth—*if* she could do it with soft talk. But murder—no."

"Who then?"

"That's what puzzles me. They say it's not Carl Hohn's

style, either. Maybe either one of them would be capable of it, if you scared them enough. I just don't know!"

"That's what comes of getting too involved in your cases, Agate Eyes. Here comes a train. Look, the boys are coming back from the graveyard, too. Watch 'em forget all about the lamented and departed victim!"

The mourners came clumping down the street, in silence except for the thud of their boots on the plank sidewalks. They heard the train, and broke into a run for their horses.

Johnny Quillen chuckled, and Hewitt looked up and saw the entire Fishhook gang riding toward them from the other side of the tracks. It was like two armies manuevering toward each other, looking for a favorable point of attack. The Fishhook crew was badly outnumbered, and for the first time, the opposition was solidly united. One murder too many, Hewitt thought . . .

The railroad station agent came out of the depot with something in his hand—what railroaders called a "hoop." It was a length of flexible bamboo about four feet long, with a circle bent permanently in one end.

Held to the other end by a spring clip was a small sheet of strong brown flimsy paper. The agent waited apprehensively beside the tracks, his eyes darting from the Fishhook riders who had pulled their horses up on the other side of the tracks, to the crowd of grim men who were just mounting up, on the street.

The train came into sight, hammering swiftly down the tracks toward them. From a hundred yards away, Hewitt could see the working of the agent's throat, as it tied itself in nervous knot after nervous knot.

"Wouldn't be surprised to see him take a leave of absence after he clears this train," Quillen murmured.

"It's possible," Hewitt conceded.

The train did not reduce speed. It would have been strange indeed if there had not been at least one boomer trainman in the cowboy crowd—somebody who knew the meaning of a hoop.

There was one. "It ain't going to stop! It ain't leaving us a goddam car! It's taking its train orders on the fly," he shouted.

No train could pass a station without written train orders, taken by wire from the despatcher's office in the last division point. The boomer in the crowd knew that the train had already been ordered not to stop at Dunsmuir. Yet it could not proceed to the next station without orders. That was the purpose of the hoop.

The conductor came down on the steps of the caboose and extended his arm. The agent hung the hoop over it "on the fly." He had removed the slip of paper and was reading his orders before he was out of sight.

The train was gone before anyone really realized it. A roar went up from the men on both sides of the track. The station agent had already started for home at a fast walk. At that roar, he burst into a run.

"Take note, Agate Eyes," said Johnny, "that Carl Hohn ain't with his crew. Where is he?"

The Fishhook crew was not to blame for the train's failure to stop—indeed, its members were more amazed than the bigger crew across the track. The Fishhook boys took one look, and saw how badly they were outnumbered.

They turned their horses and dug in their spurs. No one went after them.

Slowly, the two-hundred-odd riders who had attended the funeral straggled back to the main street. Quillen and Hewitt followed. A man in a white apron came out of a store and pointed his finger at Quillen.

"Ain't you a detective for the railroad?" he said peevishly. "What the devil's going on? I was expecting goods in yesterday. They didn't come. Now the train doesn't even stop, by the Eternal!"

Quillen waited for Hewitt to answer. "Are you one of the investors in the flour mill?" Hewitt said.

"What do you know about a flour mill?"

"I know there isn't going to be one. So does the railroad, now."

The merchant sputtered, "That's the damnedest hogwash I ever heard! The railroad has promised to put in a siding, and lease land to the mill for a dollar a year, just to get the shipping. Where did you hear that?"

Hewitt saw panic in the angry eyes. "I'm sorry. Usually, the railroad picks our pockets. Now it was almost made the sucker, and somebody is good and mad. Whoever is responsible on the railroad probably looks like a fool to his superiors. Until he gets over his hurt feelings, I don't think the line is going to worry whether Dunsmuir ever gets its goods shipped or not."

"But—but they've got one of the best milling men in the country in charge of this enterprise. He—"

"I know, he's Mr. J. Courtney Taylor of Laramie. A good many people would like to know where Mr. J. Courtney Taylor is now. He has indeed got a distinguished record—but not in the milling business. The man is a fraud and a cheat, and he's wanted for embezzlement right now."

"I don't believe you! He's due here the first of November, to meet the stockholders."

"He will not be here. Sorry, but the flimflam artists who are promoting the flour mill have been flimflammed by a master at it. How much are you in for?"

"Only two hundred, so far," the merchant said agitatedly, "but I'm borrowing more."

"Hang onto it! Don't let anybody talk you out of it. If it turns out I'm wrong, there's plenty of time to buy stock. But rest assured, I'm not wrong."

Hewitt and Quillen walked on down the street. Quillen said, "To take up where we left off, where do you reckon Carl Hohn is?"

Hewitt shrugged. "What's the difference?"

"You figger he gave the orders to gun that man down?"

"I'm sure his men did it. He was after me. The old fool no doubt blames me for the loss of his girl, and Elsie would see to it that he was kept inflamed."

Quillen said, in a troubled voice, "I dunno! I've knowed Carl for a long time. He's a hard-fisted old ignoramus, but if he wanted you dead—for the girl or any reason—he'd take a gun and try to do it himself."

"This isn't the first shot somebody had at me. I was ambushed right on the street, only they hit Ernie Hall instead. I killed a Fishhook man. One got away. I think I know which one it was."

"Before you make up your mind that Carl is hiring

killers to saw you off to a stump, I wish you'd do something for me. You come with me and talk to Carl."

Hewitt shook his head with an angry laugh. "I wish I could! His men will be shooting on sight now. That camp of his will be guarded like an army post."

"Carl won't be there. Let's go out to his place."

"How far is it?"

"Six miles. Tell you what I'll do, Agate Eyes—I swore off ever getting up on a saddle horse again. But if you're in a hurry, I'll ride out and back with you. I can't go on further than that."

"With Ernie Hall laid up, I don't like to leave the town without some kind of law officer."

"You closed the saloons. Look! Why, it's like they was a smallpox epidemic here. It'll be a ghost town today. Won't be two dollars spent in Dunsmuir this day."

The embittered men who had attended a funeral and then watched the freight train roar straight through town had not even come back to the main street. They were trotting their horses out toward the cheerless cow camps, to tend the hungry herds.

Old Bob Kramer came out as they passed the hotel. "Hidy, Mr. Hewitt, Mr. Quillen," he said. "Things has sort of quieted down. I surely did laugh to see that train puff right on through! You kind of enjoy the excitement, the first week of the shipping season. But it can get to be more trouble than it's worth after a spell."

"I expect there may be trouble over the train, don't you?" Hewitt said.

"Not today. Them boys is plumb whipped. Give them time to get over it, and they're liable to tear up that railroad. But tonight they'll just set around out there and swear at the cook."

Hewitt could trust the old man's instinct. He looked at his watch and then at Quillen. "Plenty of time for that little canter out into the country, if you're still so minded," he said.

CHAPTER TEN

They rode two of Hewitt's chestnuts—not the fastest horses in the world, in a sprint, but on the long ride, able to go and go and go. Hewitt set a hard pace. Quillen made two or three attempts to talk, but soon gave it up and devoted his efforts to sparing his big body as much punishment as possible.

For years, Hewitt had trained himself in the cold, impersonal logic that his job required. If one explanation fit the facts, and only one, then it did not matter how preposterous it seemed—that was the truth.

And now that he was out of Dunsmuir, his mind was free to grip his problem without interruption. The shape of things that forced itself on Hewitt was preposterous. An idea like this, he would have rejected angrily, no later than this morning. Yet it fit the facts—*as he knew the facts*. One did not jump to conclusions. The thing to do was talk to Carl Hohn, and see if he fit into this preposterous idea.

For a long time, they rode on Fishhook range. It was all fenced. Good-looking cattle. Range not overgrazed. Windmills pumping away beside big tanks. Fenced haystacks. The mind that had put all this together was a good one.

They rode into a ranch where the bunkhouse dominated everything. The family house was no more than a cottage, with a few shade trees and fruit trees around it. Dogs ran out to bark a welcome, scattering chickens.

Not a sign of a man on the place, but as they tied and dismounted, a woman came to the front door. Hewitt recognized the wife of the blacksmith. She was also Carl Hohn's sister-in-law, he remembered.

"What's wrong now?" she cried, hurrying toward them.

"What were you expecting wrong, ma'am?" Hewitt said.

"Nothing! He's home. That's all that counts. Why don't you leave him alone?"

"So everything's just fine, is it?" Hewitt said. She looked down at the ground, blinking away tears. He went on gently, "We're not here to make trouble. A few things have to be straightened out, and you know as well as I do that nothing will be right for your sister until we do. Where is the cantankerous old coot?"

She wrung her hands. "In the kitchen. The rocker there is the only place he can set comfortable. But please, please —don't upset him again!"

Hewitt slipped his arm around her. "You take us in, and then you and your sister let us alone for a while. You know I'm your friend, don't you?"

Hewitt had a way with women, old or young. She let him walk her to the front door, with Quillen following. Inside, it was a typical ranch house, with the kitchen the biggest and most comfortable room in the house. From it, as they entered by the living room, came voices.

"If I fried you some eggs and potatoes, would you eat them? You've got to eat something!" a woman said.

"I don't have to do anything. Let me alone!" a man snarled.

Hewitt stepped into the kitchen, carrying his hat. Hohn was propped up in a rocking chair, with his feet on a box. One glance showed that there was no fight left in him. He had become a crumpled old man, with frowsy gray whiskers and hopeless eyes.

"The Pinkerton man!" he said. "What the hell do you want? Who invited you into my house?"

The blacksmith's wife got her sister out with a glance. Hewitt threw Quillen a look. Johnny said, "Carl, you know me, surely."

"The railroad investigator," Hohn said. "What's wrong with you people? Why can't you get some cars in here?"

"We'll get to that later, Mr. Hohn," Hewitt said. "But you're in a lot worse trouble than that. Your men have committed a murder."

"If my boys killed anybody, he asked for it and it wasn't murder."

"This was cold-blooded murder. The day when you could get away with it is gone forever. Somebody's going to hang for this one."

"Who was it?"

"Circle G rider. Nobody knows his name."

"What the hell was my boys fighting with the Circle G for?"

"It wasn't a fight. They thought they were gunning me down. The victim had on my coat, and was riding a horse of mine. That's why I'm taking this matter personally."

Hewitt moved a step closer, and looked down at Hohn threateningly. "You've got at least one man with reason to want me dead. You have reason enough yourself, because I'm the man who got Mandy Rody out of town.

You'll never find her again—you or anybody else. Make up your mind to that! What I'm here for now, is to find out if that was enough to make you order your men to kill me."

Hohn had faced the fact that he was not likely to see Mandy again, but the mention of her name still hurt and shamed him. He brought his gaze up waveringly, to meet Hewitt's. "I done no such thing. If my boys killed a man, it's news to me. That suit you?"

"Not quite."

"What else do you want?"

"First, let's get the kinks out of your back. No use suffering, if I can help you. Let's get you in on the bed, lying down."

"If I could make it to the Goddamn bed, I'd be there! I can't stand to have somebody help me. It just about breaks my back in two."

"Because you probably tried to put your arms across somebody's shoulders. Let Johnny and me lift you by your belt, and see if that isn't better."

They got him to his feet without causing pain, and walked him to the bedroom. The old man was so astonished at how painless it was that he could not talk. He stood alone, while Hewitt and Quillen helped him off with his shirt and pants. He had to have help to stretch out on the bed, and then he could not move.

"Never had pain like this before," he said, almost weeping. "Old age is hell, you know it?"

Hewitt began probing gently at his spine. "I think I know what probably caused it, and it's not old age. Let me know if I hit a sore spot."

He worked in silence over Hohn's back, Quillen watching in fascination. Now and then he brought a sharp yelp of pain out of the rancher. But soon the old man began to relax. Hewitt kept kneading and pressing and twisting.

"I'm sure you know by now that there won't be any flour mill, Mr. Hohn," Hewitt said finally.

"I had my suspicions lately," Hohn said gruffly. "Our general manager was due in town two weeks ago, so him and me could set down and close the deal. He ain't showed up and I've had no word from him."

"Forget him. He never was a miller, and now he's a fugitive from justice. How deep are you in?"

"Twenty-five thousand."

Hewitt whistled. "Who got it?"

Hohn half sat up, without flinching from pain. "Nobody! You think I'm a plumb fool? The money is ready and waiting, but I didn't just hand it over to them."

"By 'them,' you mean the Devlins."

"That's right."

"Did you give them any cash at all?"

"Don't know what difference it makes now."

"There may be a chance of getting it back, sir."

"I reckon not. Elsie said it would take five thousand to bind the deal. I said the hell with that, I'd closed many a deal with a dollar binder. Well then, she said a thousand might do, so I let her have a thousand, and I made her give me a receipt for it."

"And that's all you lost?"

"No, that's when she introduced me to Mandy. Mandy wanted five thousand cash. I laughed at her. And just to show you the kind of old fool I am, less than a week later,

I was begging her to take it. I went to Topeka and bought a house for her. She wouldn't even go look at it! I finally gave Elsie Devlin the five thousand, and she talked Mandy into taking it."

"No, she didn't. Mandy didn't get a cent of it," Hewitt said. "Elsie kept telling her to save you for a really big stake. That's six thousand of your money that Elsie has. Is that all?"

"Oh—a few hundred that I gave Mandy. I don't begrudge it to her. She had a hell of a rough life. If it helps her any, I'm glad."

"Do the Devlins know that you have raised the rest of the twenty-five thousand for the flour mill?"

"Sure."

"They won't give up on it, Mr. Hohn."

"They'll never get it until I can study a deal I'm willing to sign," Hohn said bitterly. "They can go to hell and take their flour mill with them, before I'll hand over another cent to them."

"Suppose they take it away from you?"

"I've got thirty men here. I can stand off the United States Cavalry, with my crew."

Hewitt said, "But can you stand off the Devlins? They already own part of your crew. The first night I was in Dunsmuir, somebody tried to bushwhack me. Two men, and one of them nicked Ernie Hall instead. I killed one of them. The other got away."

"You don't think I had anything to do with that? Bunch of drifting riders get drunk, they're liable to—"

"This wasn't a couple of high-spirited drunks. Somebody hired them to kill me. If you didn't, who did? This morn-

ing, we buried another man killed by Fishhook men.
Gunned down without warning, after they lay in wait
for him, thinking he was me. If this is just high-spirited
horseplay, Mr. Hohn, all I can say is that your crew has a
mighty curious idea of good clean fun!"

"You think the Devlins—?"

"Who else? Suppose the Devlins take it into their heads
to take the money away from you, since they're not going
to get it any other way. Your men are all in town with
your herd. You're here, crippled up with pain, and responsible for a couple of women," Hewitt said.

"I won't ask where your money is hidden, or even how
much it is. Let's take it for granted that it's a lot, and that
it's in cash, because that's the way the Devlins do business.
But suppose I just make a guess that it's a lot more than
twenty-four thousand dollars."

"It is," Hohn grunted. "If there was money to be made
in a flour mill, I wanted as much stock as I could get."

"Does Elsie Devlin know how much it is?"

"Yes."

"How wrong would I be, if I guessed forty thousand
dollars?"

Hohn jerked his head around. "How the hell did you
know that?"

"People get into ruts, Mr. Hohn. Let's forget the money
for a minute. Tell me about Tom Black and Bill Anderson."

"Well, Tom ain't the best worker I ever had. He plays
out on me, but I think he's got the consumption and I
didn't have the heart to ride his tail. Kind of a loner. Don't
have much to do with the other men. Bill Anderson—well,

he stole Mandy from me, but I have to admit he was a real good man. Worked hard and knowed what he was doing."

"Do you remember where you hired them?"

"I was in the Royal, and Elsie said she knowed a couple of good men looking for work. Say!" Hohn narrowed his eyes and sat up suddenly, and if he felt any pain in his back, he did not show it. "Is that what you mean? That Tom is on Elsie Devlin's payroll?"

"Yes, but not for much money. Elsie can price you with a look, and Tom Black is a cheap killer. Do you think you could stand a little ride now?"

"If somebody helped me into a buggy—"

"No, I think it's the buggy that strained your back. You've been spending more time in a buggy lately than you're used to, haven't you? Get back in the saddle, and I think you'll be all right."

Hohn struggled to his feet unaided. "A man has to pay for his follies, by God! I rented a buggy to take Mandy riding. Then I decided I was too rich and important not to have a buggy and a good team of my own. And that's when my back started giving me hell! Live and learn."

"Then let us harness a team and let the women take the buggy, and saddle a horse for you. Can you find someone to keep an eye on your livestock while you're gone?"

"I've got a couple of boys out mending fence. Old skates that never saved their money, and now I've got to take care of them. Well, I saved mine, didn't I? And look where it got me! You think we ain't safe here?"

"No, I don't. I think after your wife screamed a couple of times, you'd come up with forty thousand dollars in cash in a hurry."

"Where would we be safe, though?"

Hewitt grinned. "The hotel, right under the Devlins' nose! And do me a favor, will you? Don't pay cash for anything! Run up the biggest bill you can for rooms and meals."

"Why?"

"A declaration of independence. Don't worry, they'll know what you mean! Now, Johnny will help you dress. I'll go harness a team and then saddle a horse for you, and let's light a shuck toward town."

The two women were in what was left of the summer garden, picking the last tomatoes. The blacksmith's wife hurried to meet Hewitt, as he went toward the barn.

"How is he?"

"Cheerful as a ladybug on a rose. Tell your sister she has her husband back. You both better go in and pack some clothes. They're going to have a few days at the hotel together."

"You're quite a fix-it man, aren't you?" she said.

It was after dark when they reached Dunsmuir. Carl Hohn had some pain, but he was still able to dismount at the hotel. His wife helped him up the stairs, while the blacksmith's wife went home to her own husband.

Hewitt and Quillen walked slowly toward the livery stable, leading the buggy team and the saddled horses. "Now are you satisfied that Carl had nothing to do with those killings, Agate Eyes?" Quillen said.

"I never did think he did."

"Then why did we take this damn' killing ride?"

"A man likes to be sure, Johnny."

"Sure of what?"

"Well, right now I'd like to be sure of where Tom Black is. But I'll bet we couldn't find him if we tried."

Quillen was silent a moment. Then he said, "You figger you've got your case made, don't you?"

"Pretty much."

"I've heard you say it a hundred times—close your case and take your pay and run with it! Don't get tangled up in personal feelings! Now that's exactly what you're doing, ain't it? You've earned your fee, but your fee ain't enough this time, is it?"

Hewitt did not answer. Quillen cursed long and softly. He blamed Hewitt for every ache in his big body.

At the stable, they turned the horses over to George Carrington. "Have you seen Tom Black, the Fishhook rider, around today?" Hewitt asked him.

"Not today," Carrington said. "He put his horse up here yesterday and I haven't seen him since. That don't worry me because it's Carl Hohn's horse, and he's good for the bill."

"Thank you, friend George."

They walked back to the hotel, where the clerk handed Hewitt a telegram. He opened it and read: FINISH YOUR JOB. It was unsigned, but it had been filed in Broken Bow, Nebraska.

He handed it to Quillen, who scowled over it a moment. "Now what does this mean?"

"It means I still have an expense account. Make you feel any better, Johnny? It's against the code of good conduct of our profession, to quit before the expense money is used up."

"I don't feel a damn' bit better, Agate Eyes. You're making this a personal fight."

"But now I can afford to."

"Nobody can afford to," Quillen said. "That's the way you get yourself killed, you damn' stubborn fool!"

CHAPTER ELEVEN

The next three days, in which no train stopped in Dunsmuir, were busy ones for Jefferson Hewitt. Almost no
one appeared on the street, as the hopeless, bewildered ten-
sion grew. The nearest thing to a crowd was the group
that gathered around Hewitt's fix-it shop.

Most of the work was foolish make-work. People seemed
to be drawn by instinct to him, as though sensing that
he held the key to their troubles. Hewitt remained calm
and cheerful. His night patrol as deputy marshal was now
a mere token stroll, because by nine o'clock, every light
on the street was out. He caught up on his sleep, and was
early on the job at his wagon down behind the livery
barn.

It was here Quillen found him, late on the third day. The
train had whistled through a few minutes ago—a short
passenger train that picked up its train orders on the fly,
and threw out the mail bags without stopping.

For once, there was only one client at Hewitt's stand.
A tobacco-chewing cowboy leaned against the fence with
his ankles crossed and his thumbs hooked in his gun belt,
as Hewitt drew his picture on a big sheet of paper.

Quillen watched over Hewitt's shoulder. The cowboy
was amazingly true-to-life, but he was not shown leaning

against a fence. In the picture, he leaned against a horse. Behind him was a branding fire, with a branding iron in it. The treeless skyline suggested the Kansas range.

Hewitt put his crayons down at last. "I don't suppose this is for Mother Devlin, so you won't want a poem on it, will you?" he said.

"Nope. This is for my mother, in Michigan." The cowboy came over to examine the picture. He whistled. "Yep, that's me, all right! The sheriff can use that on his 'wanted' dodgeroos, if worst comes to the worst."

"You take it easy!" Hewitt chided him. "Don't start trouble. Everything's going to work out all right."

"You keep saying that. Hope you're right. I don't have no ambition to get into a shoot-out with the Fishhook."

The cowboy paid Hewitt, rolled up his picture, and hobbled away. Quillen said, "Agate Eyes, you remind me of a fat old spider, sitting in his web and waiting for a fly to get tangled up in it."

"That one," Hewitt said, smiling. He pointed to a brown horse in the livery corral. "See that? Tom Black, *alias* Charley Kenyon, rode that horse in here. He hasn't been seen since."

Quillen nodded. "I was talking to Mrs. Devlin. She wants to make a deal."

"Do you think she means business?"

"Well, her opening offer is ten thousand dollars."

Hewitt shook his head. "She isn't serious. A bid like that is just feeling me out for a weakness, and I haven't got one. Nothing doing, Johnny!"

"You could spend years in court, and not get that much. I don't think you've got much of a case against her on the

Cushman deal, and Carl Hohn is still holding most of his money. Ten thousand for Tom Black seems like a good price to me."

"Can she deliver him?"

"Subject didn't come up."

"Bring it up. See what she says."

"Why don't you let the law take its course with him? You done the job you was hired to do, when you got that affidavit. You can collect your fee on that, can't you?"

"Yes, but you and I both know that he killed that poor nameless cowboy who was wearing my coat and riding my horse. He wasn't doing that job for Carl Hohn!"

"You think Elsie put him up to it?"

"Try her, see what she says about turning him in. Tell her I want him *only on the Broken Bow murder!* Tell her I'll dicker on money, but not on that. I get Tom Black *alias* Charley Kenyon, or there's no deal of any kind."

"All right, I'll sound her out."

Quillen plodded away. He was gone only a few minutes. He pulled up a wooden box and sat down on it, and pointed silently to the cigars in Hewitt's pocket. Hewitt handed him one and lighted it for him.

"Well, Johnny? What did the lady say?"

"First things first," Quillen replied. "Tall, thin man—say six foot three, and about a hundred and fifty—and say fifty-five years old under his dyed hair. Black mustache and blue eyes and a couple of gold teeth. Well-dressed in a good checked suit and fine boots. You'd judge him to be a bank president, except for one thing."

"What's that?"

"Oh, how that man can curse! No bank president is

going to be heard using that kind of language. First he wanted a room in the hotel, and there wasn't any. Next, he wanted to talk to Paul Devlin, but nobody can find Paul. He had to buy a good horse and saddle and put in three days riding same, because the trains ain't running. What he had to say about Dunsmuir—oh, my! Mean anything to you?"

Hewitt's pulse ran a little faster. "It might. Do you think he might be our missing flour-mill expert?"

"That thought occurred to me, yes it did."

"And he asked for Paulie, not Elsie."

"Right!"

"Did you talk to Elsie?"

"Not for long. When I told her you had to have Tom Black, like buying a frying chicken, I though she had went crazy. Agate Eyes, there's a woman at the end of her rope! She cried, she screamed, she almost got down on her knees to beg me to bring you to talk to her."

"Poor Elsie!"

Quillen frowned. "You sound like you mean that."

"I do. I've got to extract some money from her, but at the same time, I feel sorry for her."

Quillen's frown deepened. "I next expect to hear you say you're downright fond of her."

Hewitt said softly, dreamily, "There was a time that I was. Elsie's a remarkable woman, Johnny. Ambitious and greedy, and no more conscience than a tarantula. Brains enough to run the Bank of England. Only one weakness. She just isn't cold-blooded enough for the game she's playing."

"You act like you think somebody's behind her."

"I do."

"That's hard for me to figger. She fired off four telegrams to my division superintendent this week. You'd think she owned the railroad. Didn't get no answer, but she's still offended because the line won't set out the cars she demands. That don't sound like a woman who is just being used. Who is behind her?"

"Paulie."

Quillen exclaimed, "Her husband? Oh shoot, he's too yella to go home alone in the dark!"

"Yes," Hewitt said, "but smart enough, and cruel enough, to hide behind Elsie and work her like a slave! It has stared me in the face ever since I knew them in Omaha, and I couldn't see it. Johnny, who but a coward could treat a woman like that? Elsie loves to sit up there on that cashier's stool and play the stuffed Empress. She could knock a trouble-making cowboy out with a billy club and never bat an eye.

"But she's not smart enough to talk a foolish old woman out of forty thousand dollars—show her how to raise the money in cash loans at five different banks—and then murder the one man who saw through her. Seth Johnson worked for her for a long time. She knew he was crazy about her. It was kind of a good-natured joke to her.

"She could laugh at him. But she couldn't go up on the roof and push Seth off, when she saw he was wise to her. *She* knew that old Seth would never talk. He was too much in love with her.

"But Paul couldn't trust him. I knew Seth well enough to know he would never commit suicide. Somebody had to have murdered him. It was a cowardly way to do it, and that should have told me that Elsie wasn't the murderer. She hasn't got that kind of raw nerve.

"Paul has. He has the merciless nerve to try twice to have me killed, both times by Tom Black, *alias* Charley Kenyon. That's why Elsie can't deliver Kenyon—he'd rat on Paul, and both Paul and Elsie know it.

"Another thing! There was something wrong with Mandy Rody's entire attitude. She was tickled to death to get out of town. She should have been cursing the overbearing woman who got her into this mess.

"But she never said a word about Elsie! It was Paul she was afraid of, I'm convinced now, only I was too stupid to pump her on the subject then.

"Now you tell me that our absconding Laramie man is in town, looking for Paul. Not Elsie—Paul! Is there any other explanation that fits everything? You know there isn't! Nobody is as crafty and conniving as a coward. And I have been just as stupid as he thought I was."

Johnny thought it over a long time, rubbing his face with his big hands and staring at the ground. Eventually he said, "What'll you do now, go after him?"

"I won't have to. He'll come after me."

"Send Tom Black?"

"He'll try that first. When it doesn't work, he'll finally have to do the job himself."

"Suppose it does work? Black's a back-shooter."

Hewitt shook his head. "Tom Black will never get behind me. I think Elsie knows he isn't man enough for the job. Go talk to her again. Tell her it's time for her to get out from under, before the debris starts falling."

"Sh-h-h!"

A tired horse came plodding down the street and turned in at the gate. In the saddle was a tall, gaunt, distinguished-looking man with a black mustache, a head of black curls under his fine fawn-colored hat, and hard blue eyes. He wore an expensive checked suit and hand-made, flat-heeled riding boots.

Hewitt stood up. "Help you, sir?" he said.

"You can take care of my horse. Tell me where one can get a good room in this Godforsaken town. Tell me where I can find Mr. Paul Devlin. The damned, insolent ignoramus at the hotel desk turned his back on me."

"Yes sir, let me have your horse, sir," Hewitt said obsequiously. "Take your baggage too, sir?"

"Put the valise down. When I find a room, I'll send for it. I'll carry this myself," the stranger said, taking a firm grip on a fat despatch case that had hung from the horn of his saddle.

Hewitt looked at Quillen. "Boy! Take care of the gentleman's horse! Lively, now. Don't keep him waiting."

Johnny caught on fast. "Yes, sir," he said, taking the bridle reins. "Maybe the gentleman could get a room in the Hall residence, if you wrote them a note. I could take the gentleman there."

"An excellent idea!" Hewitt looked at the stranger. "A very fine couple, a merchant and his wife. I'll give them a note, introducing you. What name shall I give?"

"Mr. H. Taylor Cortwright."

"Your business connection?"

The distinguished stranger did not hesitate. "I'm with the Great Western Flour Mills."

Hewitt wrote a brief note to Ernie Hall. He was fairly sure the old marshal would understand it:

This introduces Mr. H. Taylor Cortright of Great Western Flour Mills, who was unable to secure a room at the hotel. I'm sure you will want to put him up until other arrangements can be made for his room and board.

Respectfully, Hewitt

Quillen plodded away, carrying the stranger's suitcase. Shortly, Hewitt closed his fix-it shop and walked along the empty street to the hotel. As he entered the lobby, a fat man he could not quite place accosted him.

"Mr. Hewitt, I'm staying here until some train or other stops here. Then I'm leaving town. As you said, the time comes when you have to decide. I've decided."

It was the Royal bartender that Hewitt had goaded so unmercifully. Hewitt shook hands with him. "Don't be in too big a hurry to leave. Mother Devlin may need you more than you think."

The bartender flinched. "Don't call her that! It makes her madder than anything."

"You like her, don't you?"

"I'll tell you the God's truth—I do."

"How about Paulie?"

The barkeep snorted. He called Devlin a contemptuous name, and then added hastily, "But you don't need to tell him I said that, Mr. Hewitt. Mrs. Devlin has got her good points, if you look for them. I can't think of a one that he has."

Hewitt laughed and ran upstairs to his room. He was

stretched out on the bed, completely relaxed, when Johnny Quillen's knock came at the door. Hewitt got up and let him in.

"Did Ernie find room for our tall friend?"

Quillen nodded. "He catched on quick. Say, that man sure does hang onto that despatch case, don't he?"

"There is probably upward of fifty thousand dollars in it, Johnny."

Quillen whistled. "And you're letting him keep it?"

"I'm sure he'll take excellent care of it until I'm ready to levy on him. Did you see Elsie?"

"Yes. She wouldn't even talk to me. I told you, there's a woman at the end of her rope!"

"Did you see Paulie?"

"No. But either he was around, or she was expecting him back soon. He's got her in a corner. She's got to make a deal with you, or he'll have to take steps himself. If he does, he'll take it out on her."

Hewitt nodded thoughtfully. "Johnny, looking ahead a few days, let's see how fast your railroad can get some empty cars in here. Lots of them!"

"I can already tell you that. Day after tomorrow. You figger you've got this case cleaned up?"

"Not just one case. Three!"

"Tell me something, Agate Eyes. Why did you shut off the cars in the first place?"

"When somebody is making things tough for me, I like to return the favor. When Elsie couldn't make the railroad come across with cars, she lost her standing—with Carl Hohn, with the whole town, but especially with Paulie. This was the knockout punch, Johnny."

"I see. Well, it sure knocked her out. Can I tell Carl Hohn that there will be cars day after tomorrow?"

"Yes, but tell him to keep it quiet, and tell him he's not going to hog all of them. If he tried that, there wouldn't be a Fishhook man alive by the time the train pulled out. Tell him that if he hasn't already learned his lesson, all he has to do is try to grab all these cars.

"Now go somewhere and let me sleep. I'm the deputy marshal, remember, and I've got a tour of duty tonight. Tell the bellhop to send up hot water for my bath at nine sharp."

He had shaved, bathed, and dressed, and a few minutes before ten was lighting his first cigar of the evening when he heard a soft rap at the door. He removed the chair he had propped under the knob, and opened it.

It was Bob Kramer. "Why are you all dressed to go out, Mr. Hewitt? Why don't you just stay in the hotel tonight. There ain't a soul on the street."

"What's bothering you, Bob?"

"It's a feelin', mostly. I'm an old he-coyote, and I've learned to bet my hunches. It's going to be darker than a yard down a cow's throat out there tonight, with everything closed up. You stay off the street!"

Hewitt smilingly shook his head. He locked the door to his room behind him and walked down the stairs with Kramer, chatting sociably with him. At the foot of the steps, Ernie Hall was waiting. His neck was still heavily bandaged, but if it was giving him pain, his angry face did not show it.

"Is your guest comfortable, Ernie?" Hewitt said.

Hall nodded impatiently. "Don't worry about him. He's trying to get hold of Paul Devlin, but nobody knows where Paul is. Mr. Hewitt, you ain't going out tonight, surely?"

"I see Johnny Quillen has been talking behind my back," Hewitt said. "You mustn't let Johnny worry you. He takes things too seriously."

"You give me back that badge. You're fired!"

Hewitt smilingly unpinned the badge and handed it to Hall. "I have enjoyed working for you. Now don't you think you had better go home and entertain your guest?"

Hall could only glower helplessly at his back, as Hewitt went into the dining room. The girl who always waited on him gave him an open-mouthed look of surprise.

"Good evening. Can you give me table where I can sit with my back to the wall tonight?" he said.

She looked around the crowded dining room. There was not an empty table, but it was almost a silent room. No one seemed to have anything to say to anyone. Well, he told himself, all that will change miraculously, once they start getting cattle cars again . . .

"I sure can, but you'll have to wait a minute," the girl said. "I didn't hardly expect you tonight."

"Why not?" he said smilingly.

The girl did not answer. Hewitt stationed himself where he could watch both doors, until she signaled him that a wall table was ready. "Thank you. I'm hungry tonight. I'm going to let you choose whatever is best," he said.

"That'll be the chicken and dumplings, sir."

"Sounds wonderful! Quiet tonight, isn't it?"

"Too quiet." Suddenly she leaned over the table, her

face pale, her eyes wild. "Oh, Mr. Hewitt, do you think there is going to be trouble tonight?"

"Not for you. I notice that Mr. and Mrs. Devlin aren't here tonight."

"No. She was in this afternoon, but she said she didn't feel well, and was going home."

"That's the only place to be when you don't feel well. Now, let's make you feel a little better, too."

He handed her a five-dollar gold piece. She dropped it into her apron pocket, stammered her thanks, and hurried away. She doesn't know why she's afraid, Hewitt thought, but I'll bet I do. Elsie was scared to death when she came in this afternoon. Women catch these feelings from one another. That's why there are no women gunmen . . .

Hewitt was enjoying his pie and coffee when Johnny Quillen came striding into the dining room. He sat down heavily at Hewitt's table and pointed toward the cigars in Hewitt's pocket. Hewitt gave him one and lighted it for him.

"Thanks, Agate Eyes. I went to the Devlins' house this evening. Nobody does that, I'm told, but I did. Paul came to the door. I asked for Elsie."

"And he said Elsie was ill."

"Yes. Then he just about slammed the door in my face. You can push a coward only so far, and when he's cornered, he's the most dangerous man in the world."

"He isn't cornered yet. He still has Tom Black, *alias* Charley Kenyon."

"Yes, and he ain't counting on him one damn' bit!" Quillen said passionately. "Kenyon's a ten-dollar killer, and

Paul knows it's up to him. He's finally got himself nerved up to the job. You stay off the dark streets!"

"Why? The darkness does one thing for me. It eliminates a rifle. They'll have to come at me at short range. Do you think I'm not the equal of both of them?"

"I think you're a goddam fool! This was always your weakness. You think you're smarter and colder-blooded and meaner than anybody else on earth."

"And a better shot. Don't forget that!" Hewitt stood up. "Try the chicken and dumplings, Johnny. They're superb!"

"You headstrong fool! Nobody is as good as you think you are."

"I don't think anything of the kind, Johnny, but I do like to give my adversaries the impression that I'm a deadly sort of superior killer-type. While they're worrying how to get at my weakness, if any, I'm tucking myself in safely somewhere. I'm touched that you worry, however. It's very sweet of you."

Johnny was still cursing him monotonously, in a low, despairing voice, when he went out the street door.

CHAPTER TWELVE

Not every man makes a good manhunter. He who kills to satisfy some crazed blood-lust makes a poor one because he does not even understand the job. So does the family man, however brave. So does the community leader. The qualities that make him popular rob him of the grim and lonely dedication that manhunting takes.

Hewitt was a good manhunter because he did not like to kill, and had no family ties or status in any community. He avoided risk whenever possible. When he had to take it, he tried to prepare for it by reducing the odds against him as much as possible.

The two men who were out to get him, Paul Devlin and Charley Kenyon, *alias* Tom Black, had only each other to turn to in moments of fear or indecision. Hewitt felt fairly sure that they were a frightened pair. They had no friends left.

He, on the other hand, stranger though he was, could not traverse a block in Dunsmuir without meeting someone who liked him and believed in him. It was not the first time that Hewitt has paved the way for a showdown by these methods. The decent women of the town—they were the factor that evened the two-to-one odds against him, as they always were.

Hardly a light burned in the ghost town that Dunsmuir had become since the trains no longer stopped here. Hewitt could not see a single horse tied on the main street, when at a little before ten at night, he stepped out of the hotel and began his solitary patrol. He was no longer deputy marshal here, but the decent women of the town expected him to keep the peace. Keep it he would.

He badly needed his after-supper cigar. Quillen had interrupted him at the table before he could light it, to urge him to stay off the streets tonight. Hewitt had to walk out on the railroad detective to silence him.

This was no place for a cigar. Its glowing end would blind him, while advertising his whereabouts to his enemies. He strode along, his boot heels echoing on the plank sidewalk, his spurs clinking solftly.

Other boots sounded distantly behind him. He turned and saw, at the other end of the block, three forms. He shook his head angrily. The big one would be Johnny Quillen. The others were probably the bellhop, Bob Kramer, and bullheaded old Marshal Ernie Hall.

A dim night light glowed in the Royal, but when he took a quick glimpse through a window, he saw no one inside. He rattled the locked door and walked on. In the middle of the next block, two men made darker shadows in the darkness as they leaned against a building. Whoever they were, they could not be the men he was hunting.

He stopped before them. "Aren't you boys out pretty late?"

"I don't pack a watch," said one. He stepped across the sidewalk to spit tobacco juice into the street. Hewitt saw that he wore two guns. It was the cowboy whose picture he had made today, to send back to his mother to show the life of a cowboy.

The other was the saloonkeeper who had bought the first picture and then sold it to Paul Devlin. He said, "I'm used to staying open late. Don't know what I'd do with myself if I went home."

"Boys, I advise you to get off the streets. You know why," Hewitt said, and walked on.

Behind him, the saloonkeeper said angrily, "Mr. Hewitt, you're a plain damn bonehead. Get off the street yourself! You're just begging to be killed."

A lamp burned in the office of the livery barn, but the lantern in the stable was not lighted tonight. Hewitt carefully detoured the dim light from the office window. In a moment, as he expected, he heard a voice from the dark stable.

"Mr. Hewitt, is that you?"

"Yes, George," he replied. "You're a family man, you fool! Go home to your wife and kids."

"Ain't going to be any shooting here," Carrington replied surlily. "It's always some poor horse that gets gutshot. Not this time! I'll drop anybody that comes in here packing a gun, and I won't give him a chance to draw. I'll shoot him down like a varmint."

"I suppose Tom Black has been here."

"You suppose right. His horse is saddled and ready to go."

"When did he leave here?"

"Hour or so ago, afoot. Went out the back door. You don't expect him to show himself on the street, do you?"

"Yes I do—one more time. Now go home to your family, George. A hell of a hero you make!"

Hewitt turned and started back up the street. It's nice to have friends he thought cheerfully, and for that, Mr. Jim Batchelder, I thank you. There's nothing like a lavish expense account for making friends . . .

He put his boots down more quietly now. He was half-way up the first block when a tiny metallic sound from the dark came to his ears. He froze. He even stopped breathing while he listened.

The sound did not come again, but a moment of cool thinking identified the sound for him. A railroad rail had a distinctive ring. Someone over there on the tracks had stumbled slightly in the darkness, and had let one of his spurs clink against a rail.

Well, now he knew where Tom Black, *alias* Charley Kenyon, was. It would not be Paul Devlin over there on the tracks, booted and spurred. Paulie would be out of the mud on the sidewalk. They had him between them.

Hewitt dropped to a squatting position, and studied the dim skyline over there by the tracks. No sign of the gaunt silhouette he was seeking, but his man was there. Hewitt tilted forward and, on fingertips and toes, scuttled out into the drying mud of the street.

In the middle of the street, he squatted and listened again. He turned up his coat collar and folded the lapels across his chest, to hide the small white triangle of shirt front. He slid his right hand inside the coat, and let it rest on the butt of his .45.

He was completely relaxed and unhurried. The next

move was theirs. He could crouch here all night if he had to, and they couldn't.

Time passed. He did not keep track of it, because time was on his side, not theirs. Tom Black's horse, ready for instant travel, told him that much. The murderer of Ed Batchelder meant to be out of town long before the sun rose.

Another sound came, easily identified—a stray dog in the street, startled at scenting him there. Hewitt put his hand out to it, and the dog came to him as dogs always did. He held it under one arm and stroked it, making friends. At the same time, he made sure its tail did not thump the ground to give away his position.

He let the dog lick his face until it got bored with it, and then let go of it. The dog shot its ears forward and trotted toward the track, to investigate one more stranger lurking in the dark.

Up the street, Ernie Hall shouted, "Mr. Hewitt, where are you? Are you all right, Mr. Hewitt?"

Far enough away, Hewitt thought, with satisfaction, to stay out of my affairs. Close enough to make my two bushwhacking friends a little nervous, even if Ernie is wounded . . .

Over there by the tracks, somebody's denim-clad arm rustled across the denim of his body, as he struck at the dog. The dog yelped and ran, but a dozen feet away, it stopped and barked at the top of its voice.

And kept barking, on and on. Hewitt felt better and better. That racket would drive Tom Black crazy, by giving away his position. It would force him to do something.

The fugitive began throwing cinders from the track ballast, but it only infuriated the dog more. Hewitt saw a hat bob up over the horizon and vanish. Another shower of cinders. The dog went crazy.

Hewitt pressed his gun flat against his body, to muffle the click as he cocked the hammer. He cupped his left hand around his mouth and called out jovially, "Charley, can't you shut your dog up? People are trying to sleep."

Charley Kenyon's nerves were screaming. He had sense enough to lean over and keep his profile low, as he charged the dog to silence it. But he became both a sound and a blur of movement—all the target a man needed.

Hewitt fired and threw himself forward and down. A gigantic cone of light flared toward him from the other side of the street, and the whining sigh of buckshot over his head, taught him that even Jefferson Hewitt could make a mistake. Paulie, he thought, I didn't figure you for a shotgun . . .

He twisted on his side on the ground and fired twice, quickly, at the hulking black shadow that remained on his eyelids after the glare of the shotgun blast had gone out. He heard both slugs slam into solid flesh. He heard Devlin drop the gun and collapse noisily on the plank sidewalk. He heard the awful bubbling of Paul Devlin's breath, trying to force its way through the blood that had flooded his lungs.

Over by the tracks, Charley Kenyon was whimpering softly, like a frightened child. Hewitt crept toward him, the crazed dog pointing the way. He found Kenyon's gun first, and then Kenyon.

He shouted, "I'm going to strike a match, so hold your fire!" He struck the match and made a quick examination.

"Bring a lantern," he called, "and send somebody for the doctor. This fellow is badly hurt!"

Bob Kramer came running with the lantern, Quillen only a few steps behind him. Ernie Hall ran to bring the doctor. Charley Kenyon was conscious by the time the physician got there.

"Uncanny, absolutely uncanny!" Dr. Hanrahan said, when he saw Kenyon's shattered right arm.

"No man can shoot that well," Johnny Quillen said, a superstitious quaver in his voice. "Two men shot in the dark, and both winged in the right arm. Nobody on earth can shoot that well!"

"In legends they can," Hewitt said, "and you and I know that legends are only the stories that grow up around lucky men."

By daylight, Dr. Hanrahan knew that he had to operate on the wounded man's arm. "I'm unable to stop the bleeding without surgery," he told the half-conscious patient. "I'm quite sure I'll have to cut the arm off. Do you understand that?"

Kenyon did not turn his head. "What chance did I have with that goddam Pinkerton trick shot?" he said.

The arm was off within the hour. The patient was still under the influence of the chloroform when Hewitt appeared at the doctor's house.

"I imagine that winging both of those men in the dark will enhance your reputation as a manhunter," Dr. Hanrahan said.

"You're probably right," replied Hewitt.

"I shouldn't want such a reputation, myself. Won't it

only encourage a certain type to try to kill you, just to prove it can be done?"

"That has been tried. What I came here for, however, was to talk to Mrs. Devlin. When can I?"

"For what purpose?"

"She and I have to talk business sooner or later. Postponing it doesn't make it any more pleasant."

"Can't you wait until she's over the shock of her husband's death? She loved her husband. She—"

"No, she merely lived in terror of him, that's all. Believe me, Doctor, I know! A day or two before they were married, she begged me to take her under my protection, under any terms."

"She's in a state of shock now."

"I can understand that. She can't believe she's free at last. Don't underestimate her vitality, man! Elsie has all the strength she needs, at any given time. Just ask her if she wants to talk to me, and see what she says."

Hewitt followed the doctor upstairs to the back bedroom. The doctor knocked on the door. There was nothing invalid-like about Elsie Devlin's impatient voice.

"Who is it? What do you want now?"

Hewitt smiled at the doctor and opened the door. "It's me. Dry your tears, lady. This won't take long."

"Let me get something around me, damn it!" she blazed. "All right, you bastard, come on in."

The doctor went in first, followed by Hewitt. The woman sat on the edge of the bed, wrapped in a blanket. She turned the lamp up, and its light showed Hewitt the face of an old woman. Elsie had not shed a tear, but something in her had given way like a breaking dam.

"What do you want, Pinkerton man?" she snapped.

"I'm not a Pinkerton man. Let's talk money."

She took a sack of tobacco and a paper from the bed-side table, and rolled a cigarette with a deft twist. Hewitt lighted it for her.

"Thanks," she said. "No hard feelings, Pinkerton man. It was you or him. Paul should have known better than to go up against your kind. In the long run, though, the joke is on you."

"How so?"

"I offered to deal for ten thousand. It was as high as Paul would go, and a hell of a lot higher than I'll ever go. Now you'll never get a cent."

"May I sit down?"

She nodded. Hewitt sat down on the edge of the bed beside her. The doctor watched with a puzzled frown.

"What makes you think I'll never get a cent? I'll collect for Charley Kenyon. I'll collect for J. Courtney Taylor."

She stared at him. "For who?"

"Your flour-milling expert. He seems to have stolen half the money in Laramie. There's a five-thousand-dollar reward. I turned him in to Ernie Hall. Ernie has him in custody."

She continued to stare at him stupidly. He went on, "He came to see you, Elsie, but I saw him first. This is what happens when a gambler gets a streak going. Now I'm free to devote all my attentions to you."

"Court stole money in Laramie?" she got out, at last. "That dumb son of a bitch hasn't got sense enough to pull off a job by himself! And then, like a fool, he came here, did he?"

"Yes, you have bad luck in your partners, don't you? Paulie made life hell for you. Carl Hohn turned out to be stubborn about handing over his money. Mandy Rody ditched the whole proposition for a man her own age. It leaves you—"

"A widow," she cut in, "and I'll keep what I have. Pinkerton man, you've got as much chance of getting money out of me as a celluloid dog chasing an asbestos cat through hell!"

"Where you have made your mistake all along," he said, "is in being so sure I'm a Pinkerton man, on a salary. I'm not. I have a partner, one of the best accountants in the business. He's already on his way. We work on a percentage of recovery. The more we find of the Cushman money, the more we make. The courts will have to probate Paulie's estate. Everything will come out then.

"My partner and I can stay here as long as we have to. You can keep everything you've made in the last five years, but we want the forty thousand that you took from old Mrs. Cushman. My partner is greedy about money, but the thing that counts with me, Elsie, is that *Seth Johnson was my friend!* Paulie pushed him off the roof, didn't he?"

"If he did—"

"Elsie, you know he did!"

"Well," she flared, "I didn't know it at the time. If I'd said anything, he'd've killed me, too."

"I believe you, but you're still not going to make money out of Seth's death. I'll settle for the forty thousand for the

Cushman heirs, if I can. If I can't, I'll stay here as long as it takes to pick you like a chicken. And you know by now that I can do it, don't you?"

Her face crumpled, and she seemed to age another ten years. She lay down on her face on the bed and began weeping for the first time since her husband's death. "Oh God, I'll have less than twenty thousand dollars. If you'd only run off with me, Pinkerton man, before Paulie made me marry him! We'd make a good pair, wouldn't we?"

"Yes, we would," Hewitt said, rising. "With your brains and my looks, we could go far."

"Oh, go to hell!" she snarled.

CHAPTER THIRTEEN

Hewitt spent a week and a half in Broken Bow, Nebraska, with the temperature near zero every day he was there. In the long run, the cold wave made the job easier. A freak of nature made the dead horse clearly visible under the ice.

The sheriff's crew spent a day hacking it out of the ice. No question but what it was Ed Batchelder's horse and saddle—no question about the bullet wounds that Slim Gurkey's affidavit said would be there.

Digging the gun out of the frozen ground was hard work, but it was where Slim had said it would be. The sheriff reopened the inquest. Hewitt was the first witness called. Before the coroner's jury could vote on a verdict, Jim Batchelder asked permission to speak.

"It has cost me close to twenty thousand dollars to clear my name. I reckon now that I'm entitled to inherit my brother's property. As long as it's mine, that woman of his can live there free of charge. She was the one that spent Ed's money faster than he could make it," the old man said.

"I bear no grudge against anybody, not even the fella that shot Ed. Setting there in that Kansas jail, a one-armed man, waiting to see whether he's extradited to stand trial or dies of consumption first, that seems to be punishment enough. I'm only grateful to Mr. Jefferson Hewitt, that he was able to clear my name so cheap. I told him he could go as high as thirty thousand, and he only spent twenty!"

It was colder than ever when Hewitt reached Cheyenne, the week after Christmas. He went straight from the train to the Bankers' Bonding and Indemnity Company, where a burly, nearsighted man with a stern mouth in a pink, bland face greeted him as though he had only returned after a trip to the corner for a beer.

"You took your time getting back, Jefferson. Have a case in Montana for you. Thirty thousand missing. We can get fifty percent of recovery."

Hewitt shook his head. "I'm going to take some time off, Conrad. I'm weary to the depths of my soul."

"It's the women, Jefferson. Women wear you out, with your emotional nature. First Elsie Devlin, then Mandy Rody, and I don't know who else."

"No one else. Before we proceed one step further, we ought to settle up on the cases we've just completed. I feel I'm still short considerable money, Conrad."

"I don't see how you figure that."

"Well, here's how I have it worked out on paper," Hewitt said. "I'm not an accountant. But two and two still make four. This seems rather simple to me."

He put a paper on Conrad's desk. The partner picked it up and frowned over it:

Recovery in Cushman case (30% of $29,500)	$ 8,850.00
Recovery for Carl Hohn (50% of $3,200)	1,600.00
Fee in Batchelder case	5,000.00

Reward for J. Courtney Taylor   5,000.00
Total income from cases $20,450.00
   LESS EXPENSES:
     To John Quillen, his fee $2,000.00
     To Amanda Rody,
       balance   500.00   2,500.00
Net profit to be divided
   by partners $17,950.00
Share of Conrad Meuse   8,975.00
Share of Jefferson Hewitt $ 8,975.00
Received by Jefferson Hewitt so far   6,115.00
   STILL DUE TO JEFFERSON HEWITT $ 2,860.00

"I had some expenses for my trips to Omaha and Kansas," Conrad said coldly, "and you know how I hate to travel on trains and live in hotels."

"Yes," Hewitt said, "and I know how you keep books on expenses. Those are all charged off here in the office."

"Well, but you had four fine horses, a wagon, and some tools. Worth a lot of money! What became of them? Why did Quillen get so much? You had already got rid of the Rody girl—why send her any more?"

Hewitt's heart began to beat, the way it had beat when the teacher had him on the carpet down in that country school in the Ozarks.

"I paid Mandy, because she wrote to Carl Hohn that I was cheating her. There wasn't much else I could do. I paid Johnny because we may need him again," he said.

"But the horses and wagon?"

"You know how women are, Conrad."

"I'm afraid I don't. How are they?"

Hewitt gulped. "Elsie Devlin took a fancy to them. You

saw the shape the Devlin books were in! We couldn't have proved a thing without a court-supervised audit. That would have taken two years, at least. Elsie wants to take a long trip this spring. She agreed to sign over the twenty-nine thousand, five hundred, if I'd forget the rest and give her the house wagon and teams. It was a money-making deal, Conrad."

"You mean you *gave* them to her?"

"They didn't cost anything. They were paid for out of my expense account."

"They were still the property of this firm."

Hewitt took out his handkerchief and wiped his face, which glistened with nervous perspiration. "There are some things a gentleman can't do. He can't cheat a woman —Mandy Rody, for instance. And when he has just killed another woman's husband, he can hardly deny her a couple of teams and a wagon . . ."

Hewitt came out of the interview with his partner better than he had expected. At least, he had not given up as much as he usually did. He had Conrad's check for $2,500 to deposit in the bank.

The president of the bank saw him come in, and greeted him smilingly. "Ah there, Mr. Hewitt! Delighted to see you before you leave for Montana, and lucky you came in at this time. There's someone I want you to meet."

"I'm not going to Montana," Hewitt said brusquely. "Any time they offer you half the recovery, you can bet there isn't going to be anything recovered."

A woman stood up suddenly beside the president's desk, with a woebegone look on her face—the loveliest face

Hewitt had seen in years and years. Blue eyes, fair skin, tumble of yellow curls under a fetching knitted cap. Big, kissable, sweet-looking mouth. Wonderful figure, and the kind of clothes that showed taste and judgment, not just money.

"Not going to Montana?" she wailed. "Oh dear, but Mr. Meuse promised you would!"

"Oh. Oh, are you the client from Montana?" Hewitt said stupidly.

The bank president bowed. "Mrs. McTavish, may I present Mr. Hewitt? Jefferson, this is Mrs. Corinne McTavish. Her husband was murdered when their mine was looted. I introduced her to Conrad Meuse. I'm afraid I was counting on you to help her, myself."

Hewitt bowed over her lovely little hand, as she said, "Every cent we had in the world. Thirty thousand dollars! I've been working in a restaurant here, until you could get back. Everybody says you're the man I need to get my money back."

There are some things, the former Ozark boy said to himself, that a gentleman can't refuse. "At least we can go somewhere and talk about it, Mrs. McTavish," he said. "May I have the honor to offer you luncheon?"